What the critics are saying...

"Sex Kittens is an extremely erotic and intriguing anthology. The stories revolving around the transformation of cats into humans are not only very believable, but they are just plain fun!" ~ *Sarah W. for The Romance Studio*

"Don't miss out on this book. Two great authors couldn't have created a better paranormal erotic anthology like this one." ~ *Melinda, Enchanted in Romance*

Rating 4/5 "Once again the capricious gods and their antics are the highlight of a delightful story where humans serve as entertainment to the gods. This time Jupiter and Venus." ~ *Miaka chase, Heat Level H, Just Erotic Romance Reviews*

"Sex Kittens lives up to its titillating name with a wonderfully sexy tale. Don't miss the fun and adventure with Sex Kittens." ~ *Patti Fischer, Romance Reviews Today*

4 Hearts "Sex Kittens is an extremely erotic and intriguing anthology. The stories revolving around the transformations of cats into humans are not only very believable, but they are just plain fun!" ~ *Sarah W. for The Romance Studio*

"Sex Kittens lives up to its titillating name with two wonderfully sexy tales. Don't miss the fun and adventure with Sex Kittens." ~ *Patti Fischer for Romance Reviews Today*

D0170340

Sex Kittens has two hot stories that will tease readers' senses. Erotic tension runs through them and the sexual situations will raise temperatures! There is plenty of humor infused into these stories and many of the situations will bring forth a smile or laugh. The common theme is a beloved pet becoming a full-fledged human female. Those readers, who enjoy paranormal romance with intense sexual situations, will find this book is right up their alley. Readers will be thoroughly entertained by both stories. ~ *Susan for Loves Romances*

"Don't miss out on this book. Two great authors couldn't have created a better paranormal erotic anthology like this one." ~ *Melinda, Enchanted In Romance*

4 Heat Level: "Pussyfooting Around was an entertaining read. I especially enjoyed the very realistic portrayal of what would likely happen if a cat turned into a woman and tried to learn how to adjust and adapt in." ~ *Miaka Chase Rating: H Just Erotic Romance Reviews*

SEX
Kittens

Ashley Ladd
Myra Nour

ELLORA'S CAVE
ROMANTICA PUBLISHING

An Ellora's Cave Romantica Publication

www.ellorascave.com

Sex Kittens

ISBN #1419952234
ALL RIGHTS RESERVED.
Cat Maiden Copyright© 2004 Myra Nour
Pussyfooting Around Copyright© 2004 Ashley Ladd
Edited by: Sue-Ellen Gower and Briana St. James
Cover art by: Syneca

Electronic book Publication: November, 2004
Trade paperback Publication: October, 2005

Excerpt from *Civil Affairs* Copyright © Ashley Ladd, 2004
Excerpt from *As You Wish* Copyright © Myra Nour, 2004

Warning:

The following material contains graphic sexual content meant for mature readers. *Sex Kittens* has been rated *E-rotic* by a minimum of three independent reviewers.

Ellora's Cave Publishing offers three levels of Romantica™ reading entertainment: S (S-ensuous), E (E-rotic), and X (X-treme).

S-*ensuous* love scenes are explicit and leave nothing to the imagination.

E-*rotic* love scenes are explicit, leave nothing to the imagination, and are high in volume per the overall word count. In addition, some E-rated titles might contain fantasy material that some readers find objectionable, such as bondage, submission, same sex encounters, forced seductions, etc. E-rated titles are the most graphic titles we carry; it is common, for instance, for an author to use words such as "fucking", "cock", "pussy", etc., within their work of literature.

X-*treme* titles differ from E-rated titles only in plot premise and storyline execution. Unlike E-rated titles, stories designated with the letter X tend to contain controversial subject matter not for the faint of heart.

Contents

Cat Maiden

Myra Nour

Prologue

The gods were once disputing whether it was possible for a living being to change its nature. Jupiter said "Yes," but Venus said "No." So, to try the question, Jupiter turned a Cat into a Maiden, and gave her to a young man for a wife. The wedding was duly performed and the young couple sat down to the wedding feast.

"See," said Jupiter, to Venus, "how becomingly she behaves. Who could tell that yesterday she was but a cat? Surely her nature is changed?"

"Wait a minute," replied Venus, and let loose a mouse into the room. No sooner did the bride see this than she jumped up from her seat and tried to pounce upon the mouse. "Ah, you see," said Venus. "Nature will out."

Chapter One

"Nature."

"Nonsense," Jupiter thundered.

"Nature will out." Venus insisted, rending the heavens with a bolt of lightning.

* * * * *

Antonius stared at the storm brewing outside. Lightning and thunder crashed. The gods were angry about something. He squinted through the lashing raindrops, watching for a small form at the edge of the woodlands. Madria, his cat, was out there.

Shaking his head, he closed the door. He'd not wanted to let her out when the wind started whipping furiously, but her strident meows had persisted until he opened the door. His cat ran past him swiftly into the dark night, a strong will encased in a streaking flash of black fur.

Keeping one ear cocked for her scratch upon the door, Antonius ran his hands over the new lump of clay. His intent was to make a statue, but what form would take shape he couldn't say yet. He let the material speak to him before starting the shaping between his hands.

So far, this clay had sat as still as the rock fence around his garden. Silent.

Thrusting one hand through his hair, he shrugged. It would come. He was just surprised. Never before had it taken days for the material to make its true form known to him.

Deciding to ignore the lump of mud for a bit, Antonius pulled a bowl of chickpeas into his lap and shelled them. The storm raged, as if the gods were truly in the midst of a great battle. Lightning flashed, making it seem almost daylight inside his house, while thunder shook the rafters overhead. He shivered. The temperature dropped as the rain poured down. The howling wind pushed with insistent violence beneath the door and around the window edges. He became concerned for Madria's safety. Usually, she hunted for a mouse or lizard quickly, returning triumphant with the small prey clutched in her mouth. Perhaps she'd taken shelter beneath an overhanging tree.

His neighbor and friend, Decimus, laughed at his attachment to a mere cat, but to Antonius she was more than that. She was a constant companion, except when she hunted.

Madria stayed by his side while he tended his garden and followed in his tracks when he strolled through the woods. Most noticeably, she sat and watched each new creation he carved.

He knew Madria could not truly appreciate the beauty of his statues, but she seemed fascinated by the process. Or perhaps she simply enjoyed his company too.

Antonius led a solitary life. His parents had died years ago, leaving this humble abode. Two siblings had died soon after their birth. The few neighbors surrounding him were also friends, but each led the busy life of farmers, and all had families.

Decimus had married last year and seemed most happy. He joked with Antonius about his carefree ways, but truly, Antonius also wished to wed. But as yet, he'd not met a maiden who set his heart on fire.

He glanced in the corner where he kept a tiny statue he'd made last year. He sold all his other creations, but he couldn't part with the delicate beauty of the feminine form. The suppleness of the feline body had been carved into the gentle, yet firm lines of the statue's curving waistline. The hint of muscularity beneath the stone flesh defied the fuller, voluptuous statues that were so popular. Her hips were slim, made more for running marathons than carrying babies.

The breasts were small and pert, unlike the more pendulous breasts found on most statues. Her legs were slender too, not the thick-limbed fullness of a farm girl. Certainly, if he had used a model for his creation, she would not have been from the servant class. Not quite aristocratic either. Somewhere in between.

He sighed. Maybe therein lay his difficulty. He waited for a maiden as lovely as his creation.

Antonius smiled wryly. He doubted that would ever come to pass. There were comely maids in the villages nearby, but none came close to matching the lithe form he'd carved. Most were big-busted with wide hips, and although they were attractive, they were not what he saw as the feminine ideal.

He'd studied nature to imbue realism into his art. The gentle sway of a weeping willow became transposed into the graceful arch of a girl's body. A doe's long-lashed beautiful eyes were recreated in the lovely eyes of a statue.

Maybe that's why Madria fascinated him so much. He had tried to capture her sleek beauty and carve it into a female form, but failed each time, finally giving up. The delicate statue was the closest he'd come to recreating the feline's sleek form.

The fire in the small hearth crackled and Antonius glanced up from his musings. Was that a scratch at the door?

Jumping up, he pulled the door open, sucking in his breath as a body fell across the threshold. A woman. A nude woman.

He knelt and shook her shoulder, but she didn't stir. Carefully, he edged his hands under her and pulled her limp weight into his arms. She was surprisingly light in spite of her unconscious state.

Stretching her out on his bed, Antonius grabbed an extra blanket and rubbed the dampness from her skin. She was soaked, her long black locks sticking to her body.

He tried to stay detached as he dried her, but it was difficult. She was the most perfect specimen of womanhood he'd ever seen. Clenching his jaw, he ignored his pounding cock.

Her skin looked like the texture of a ripe peach, soft and velvety, while the color was a pale, creamy beige. Her body was petite and delicately made, the breasts modest-sized and tipped with dark rose nipples. On her slim form, the size was just right, in his estimation.

He dried a spot near her waist. It dipped in tightly, then flared out to slim hips. When he eased her onto her stomach, small, round buttocks were revealed. Antonius' heart pounded. How he wished he could stroke her silken skin in lust instead of like a nursemaid.

As he moved the blanket downward, his eyes followed its trail. Her legs were finely formed, even her feet delicately shaped.

Antonius finished drying her, then turned her gently onto her back. He covered her with the remaining blanket, and spread her long hair out to dry. He examined her face—oval-shaped with high cheekbones, set off with dramatically winged eyebrows that slashed like black wings across her brow. Complementing her features were full pink lips, giving her face an exotic air, as if she were not human but a mythical creature.

He shook his head at his fancies. Then he shook her shoulder gently, but she still did not stir. Thick, long black lashes lay against her creamy flesh. It was a startling, lovely contrast. What color would her eyes be? He was tempted to lift one eyelid, but resisted. He wanted her to look at him with clarity the first time he gazed into her eyes.

The girl sneezed and Antonius became worried. A cold would be unpleasant, but the liquid that rattled in the lungs could be deadly. Picking up the blanket he'd dried her with, he dabbed at the thick strands of her hair. She shivered violently.

Jumping up, he placed more broken branches into the hearth, heating the small house swiftly. Although spring nights were chill in northern Italy, a large blaze quickly overheated the one room. It was just what she needed, but he was soon sweating. Continuing to dry the mystery woman's hair, he became more worried as her shivers continued.

Antonius knew what he had to do. Stripping quickly, he crawled into the tiny bed and pulled her limp body into his arms. She mumbled, then snuggled against him. He was in an infernum. It was so hot, sweat poured from him. And a heavenly goddess lay clutched in his arms, her sleek curves seeming to fit every line.

Thankfully, her shivers quickly subsided. Antonius was startled when a thrumming shot through his body. Puzzled, he glanced around him, then down at the woman. She was still unconscious, but the strange movement emitted from her. If it were Madria his hands rested upon, he would say it was purring. But she was human, wasn't she?

Chapter Two

Antonius must have fallen asleep, for the next thing he was aware of, wetness coated his chin.

"Madria?"

His eyes popped open as he spoke. He expected his cat to be lazing atop his chest, kissing him awake with her tongue as she loved to do.

The ethereal black-haired beauty met his gaze. Her upper body was propped on his chest, and her lovely eyes stared into his.

Green. A brilliant spring-green color. He'd only seen such a hue on one other creature—Madria.

Vibrations tickled his chest. Antonius was sure this time that the sensation was a purr that emitted from the woman. He shivered, wondering if he were indeed faced by an unearthly being.

Realizing he'd been staring at her while his thoughts flew about, he asked, "Who are you?"

She smiled, a soft stretching of her full lips that gave her a self-satisfied look.

"You said my name before."

Her voice was low, with an accent that was extremely sexy.

"Madria?"

She nodded, her eyes twinkling.

"That's my cat's name too." He stared at the lush inky locks falling like silk around her shoulders. The name suited her. It was a Greek name meaning dark.

"Are you Greek?"

She shrugged those delicate shoulders, a blank expression coming over her expressive face. If she wished to stay secretive about her origins, he would comply.

"You took care of me."

Her simple statement broke through his thoughts.

"Of course."

She leaned down and rubbed her silken hair against his face. "Thank you," she whispered near his ear, then flicked the lobe with her warm tongue.

His cock jumped to immediate attention and he hoped she wouldn't notice. "You're welcome."

Madria moved under the cover and Antonius held his breath when she adjusted her body completely over his. She shifted her lower body, her soft pubic hair brushing against his hardness. No way could she ignore his erection.

She stared at him, barely blinking as she gently moved her hips. He couldn't hold back a groan as her slick, warm pussy lips slipped up and down his cock, the slow rhythm tempting him with the delights awaiting him within.

Gathering all the resolution and strength he needed as an artist, he took her shoulders in his hands. "Madria, you must stop."

"Why?" Her lips pursed in a pout while her green eyes glowed. Wicked orbs, full of hidden knowledge.

"You...I just found you outside, exhausted and soaked to the bone." He moved one hand to her head and felt around gently. "Perhaps you struck your head."

When his hand moved toward her mouth, she turned sideways, licking his skin. He flinched beneath her body, as if she had stroked the whole length of him. His cock throbbed within the wet heat of her lower lips.

"Does one have to be sick or crazy to mate?"

"No, I—" he paused, not even sure what he wished to say. How did you reply to such logic? And her usage of the word "mate" threw him. It wasn't a term young maidens normally used.

"But, I don't even know you." Why was he arguing with the most gorgeous woman he'd ever seen and, more importantly, trying to talk her out of sex?

"Don't you?" That purring sound vibrated through his body again and she rubbed her nose against his.

The whole situation seemed insane. Or perhaps some dread disease was ripping through his body, disorientating his senses, for there was a feeling of familiarity about this luscious creature driving him mad with desire. Had he met her in one of the nearby villages?

Her head returned to his ear and she slowly tongued it and breathed warm air into it, while her pussy continued to slide up and down his cock, driving him to distraction with the burning need to finally thrust inside and fill her with his length. Forget whether they'd met and where—she knew what she wanted. And he'd never been on fire for a woman as much as he was at that moment. His cock ached and he hoped he wouldn't climax before even testing the delights of her inner secrets.

Running his hands through her lustrous locks, he brought her face toward him. A quick flick of her pink tongue to his nose was nice, but it wasn't what he wanted.

When he pulled her lips to his, her whole body went still. Opening his eyes, Antonius was enchanted by her quizzical stare. He edged her mouth open and stroked her tongue with his. Those gorgeous eyes became excited and she lapped at his tongue in return.

He thought it was charming that Madria seemed to never have experienced a kiss. But as their kiss deepened and she followed his lead with enthusiasm, he wondered briefly about the contradiction in her actions.

She wanted sex and had acted the bold seductress. Yet, she'd never kissed before? It seemed a mad concept.

When she positioned her pussy so that his cock slid inside her slick, hot depths, he forgot all inconsistencies and questions. His hands caressed the velvety skin of her ass and shoved her down upon his hardness. Here was reality — Madria's hot flesh.

"Oh, oh, oh." Madria flung her hair wildly, whipping the silken strands across his face. Her channel gripped his cock, squeezing it so powerfully it felt like a hand milked him.

His blood boiled and his engorged flesh screamed for release. Grabbing her head, Antonius brought Madria back to his lips, drawing upon the nectar of her mouth. She plunged down strongly upon him. His cock swelled more and Madria whimpered in reaction. Her tongue darted swiftly between their joined lips, and then she sucked his lower lip into her mouth. It was too much, her hot kiss throwing him over the edge. With a loud groan, he stiffened as his sperm gushed into her slick channel.

After the last of his fluid pumped out, she stretched out on him, her sweet breath fanning his neck. He caressed her smooth back. "I'm sorry, it's been a while since I made love...and you were so damn hot."

Madria rose up and faced him. "Don't worry, my sweet Master. We have all the time in the world." She stroked one hand down the side of his face.

Antonius did not understand why she called him master, but he wasn't going to ask. Perhaps it was a slip of the tongue. Was Madria a runaway slave?

"Are you hungry?"

"Starved." She nodded quickly.

He jumped up and gathered a few items, bringing them back to the bed. She took a hunk of bread and large slice of cheese from him.

"No meat?" She took a small nibble from the bread.

"Afraid not." He watched her eat, her movements dainty. "Do you like bread and cheese?"

"Yes." She licked a crumb from her bottom lip. "But there is nothing like ripping into flesh."

Antonius' stomach did a flip. She made it sound almost savage.

"I can catch us fish tomorrow."

"Wonderful. I do love fish." A soft purring erupted from her.

He couldn't believe what she did when she finished the last bite of cheese. She licked her fingers over and over, but never wiped them on the blanket. Madria kept at her fingers until they gleamed. Afterward, she swiped the back of her hand with that pink tongue and cleaned her face using the wetness from her hand.

A shiver ran down his back. Not a human gesture. Surely, she must be some mythical creature. Maybe a wood nymph? He'd heard they were very earthy beings, and loved sex in a wild, natural way. Perhaps their grooming habits would be animalistic as well.

Shrugging, Antonius decided he didn't really care. Madria had made no moves that indicated she wished him harm. In fact, she seemed downright affectionate toward him.

Whatever she was, he'd made up his mind to keep her…at least, until she decided to leave. At that moment, she seemed most content to stay with him.

Pausing in her cleaning, she yawned widely. He was struck with the brilliant whiteness of her teeth, unlike some beauties whose looks were spoiled by decaying teeth. They looked strong too, like she could bite through meat easily.

Blinking slowly, she curled up in the middle of the bed, pulling the blanket around her, making a nest of sorts.

Antonius stretched out beside her, face to face with her. Her drowsy eyes made him extremely sleepy as well. His last glance was at her peacefully sleeping face, completely relaxed in his presence, while a soft purr rose at every breath.

Chapter Three

Antonius was awakened by the bed moving. Opening his eyes, he was surprised to find Madria doing some kind of strange dance upon the covers. Or at least that's what it looked like. She was on her back, scraping her skin into the wool blanket, her head flung backward toward the wall.

It was still pitch-black outside, but the fire in the hearth lit the interior enough for him to see her body quite well.

"What are you doing?"

She seemed startled, her gaze coming down and capturing his eyes. She stretched, her whole body going taut and pulling her cute breasts upward.

"Just feeling alive."

He chuckled.

She flipped over to her stomach and then to her knees. Her wild locks fell all around her. She looked primitive and so sexy it was unreal.

"And I am horny."

He cleared his throat before speaking. "Really?" It had to be true—his climax had been swift. Surely she had not found release.

Madria had reached his face and she leaned down for a sultry kiss. He was surrounded by the dark cloud of her thick hair. It was like being encased in a silky fall of fabric. His cock engorged in response.

She smelled wonderful, like the earth after a cooling rain shower and her warm mouth tasted of cheese. He stroked her tongue, his heart speeding up in excitement as her tongue slid in and out with sensuous flexibility. For someone who appeared to never have been kissed before today, she had the erotic expertise of an experienced lover.

She withdrew and gave him that wicked look.

"You like to lick?"

"Sure, what did you have in mind?" His voice came out a hoarse whisper.

She edged upward, until one pert breast hung over his face. He wrapped one hand around that plump mound as his splayed hand caressing her back pulled her body forward.

When he took the swollen nipple into his mouth, she sighed. He loved the texture of the pebbled skin beneath his flicks. Loved the way her breath increased as he tongued her sensitive nipple. When he nipped at her flesh, she gasped and arched upward.

Antonius desired her as no woman before her. Madria seemed to strike at his lustful core, allowing him to indulge his artistic senses to their fullest. His sensitive fingertips picked up every nuance of her flesh, and his eyes noted every perfection of her slender form.

He flipped her over onto her back and spent some minutes giving each breast attention. Madria's rosebud nipples called to him and he suckled them for long seconds, enjoying their stiff texture. She reacted with little moans, thrusting her round globes toward him. Smiling to himself, Antonius responded to her silent plea, pulling her tight flesh further into his mouth and applying more pressure on it. Her skin was cool in contrast to the heat of his mouth. His cock pounded with pulsating blood and he ached to be inside her. But not yet.

As he started to trail kisses down her satiny skin, Madria pushed him off her body then repositioned herself on her knees.

"Make love to me like this." She stared at him through the curtain of her hair, her eyes feral. "Like animals do," she said huskily.

How could he refuse such a request? Simply, he was reluctant to refuse her anything and, shaking his head at his wayward thought, sat up and ran his hands along her back. She arched upward, apparently enjoying the massage.

"Hmm, oh yes, that feels so good." Her words came out slowly, with a purring sound between each one.

Her cute ass rose up each time his hands stroked down her round cheeks. Positioning himself behind her knees, he kissed the ultra-soft skin of her butt.

Gripping one cheek, he kneaded it with both hands, then leaned down and licked her flesh. The velvety texture beneath his tongue was delicious and as lush as the peach he'd compared it to when he first observed her delicate skin. He laved one long stroke along the crease between her cheeks. She moaned and shoved backward. He chuckled.

Antonius nibbled at her delicate skin, enjoying the salty, womanly taste of it. His cock throbbed with the need to plunge into her moist depths.

He took a large mouthful of yielding flesh and, using his tongue, stroked the captured skin. He wanted to bite her all over.

"Meow."

He stilled in his licking bites, startled by her meow. But then she wiggled her ass and he disregarded that strange exclamation.

Holding his aching cock, he edged it into the hot opening of her pussy. She purred loudly and her body went completely still. He moved slowly inside, groaning at the exquisite sensation of her slick flesh welcoming him with little grasping motions.

He backed out and rammed into her with one stroke and Madria exhaled a big breath. As he settled into a rhythm of slow strokes interspersed with long, hard ones, she panted and moved her hips in a circular rotation.

Stopping her movements abruptly, she demanded, "Come here, over my back." Her voice brooked no argument.

Not that Antonius would choose to argue with such a command. From his position kneeling behind her, he stretched his body over hers. His hand reached underneath, gently squeezing a breast while he shoved into her pussy.

"Yes," she said huskily. "Now, bite my neck."

Leaning down, he flipped her long tresses to the side, licked the side of her elegant neck, then gave it a nibble.

She exhaled a breath. It had a frustrated edge to it.

"No. Bite the back of my neck and keep my skin in your mouth."

Now he got it. She wanted to mate like cats when they were in heat. More specifically, she wanted to be held like the male cat held the female while he fucked her. As he flipped her hair to either side of her neck, clearing the back of it, Antonius was more convinced than ever that Madria had an animalistic nature. Either that, or she had a fetish for being bitten on the back of the neck.

It took a minute for him to position his mouth, but he managed to take a large portion of soft flesh and hold it with a wide-open bite.

"Yes!" she screamed, lunging her hot pussy backward, slamming herself over his engorged cock.

Saliva leaked from his mouth, but Antonius ignored it and plunged into her wet, eager flesh with force.

Her mewling response set his loins on fire and sent the blood pounding through his cock. His orgasm was coming, as fierce as the primitive, lustful sensation that gripped his body in a hard vise. Releasing her neck, he threw his head backward, the rest of his body taut as his climax thundered through his body.

"Argh," he bellowed as his cock gushed his seed powerfully into her.

"Antonius," she screamed, her whole body trembling as her hot flesh convulsed around him.

After the last of his sperm flowed out, he eased out of her and they fell onto the bed, her body spooned into his. He cuddled Madria in his arms, overwhelmed with emotions he had a hard time putting a name to. The joy rushing through his body felt like love. But that was impossible—he'd just met this wondrous girl.

Antonius had just had the best sex of his life—that must account for this odd sense of happiness and contentment.

He gently stroked her arms. She wiggled against his length like a kitten seeking to find the best spot for a nap. Her gentle breathing soothed him somehow and the thrumming sensation of her purr pulled him down with her into sleep.

Chapter Four

Antonius awoke feeling so good. He stretched and was startled when his arm bumped into something. Turning, he was face to face with the charming waif he'd found last night. He grinned. In his drowsy state, he'd forgotten about her.

Madria's sleepy-eyed blinks and then wide yawn, made him chuckle. How could he forget, for even a few seconds, such an unusual woman?

"Morning, sleepy."

"Morning." She stretched, pulling her whole body into a taut line. "I like your bed."

Stroking one lock of her hair, he asked, "How are you feeling?"

"Wonderful." She propped up on one elbow and her gaze flitted around the room. She cocked her head, listening.

"Just the mice in the rafters." He caressed her arm. A loud growling drew his eyes back to her. Madria's stomach was protesting loudly, while she stared intently at the ceiling.

"I'm hungry."

"Of course." He jumped up, then brought the leftover cheese and bread to the bed.

Madria took the proffered pieces, her expression bored.

Antonius received the distinct impression she was thinking of something else for breakfast. Where did she come from? Bread was often the breakfast of necessity around these parts. He had been lucky and bartered with a neighbor recently to acquire the large hunk of goat cheese.

"I promise — fish for supper."

She smiled happily then and ate what he gave her.

After breakfast, Antonius went through his morning wash up, and watched Madria superstitiously. She tried unsuccessfully to rake her fingers through her hair.

"Here." He handed her a comb.

Her attempts with the comb were clumsy, and she kept tangling the locks in the teeth of the comb. He reevaluated his earlier thought about her being a runaway slave. Maybe she was a maid with wealth, used to getting her hair brushed by a servant?

Taking the comb from her, he worked on the tangled mass. After some minutes, the locks fell in a silky curtain down her back. Purrs emitted from her the whole time. Antonius shook his head and finished the task. By now he was used to her purring, but her origins were still a mystery.

"Done."

"It feels good." She patted the ends. Her eyes were even more drowsy than when she awakened.

Taking his good linen tunic, the one he saved for trips to town, he handed it to her. "You can wear this."

Antonius started for the door, calling over his shoulder. "I'm going to work now. You can rest." Before his hand reached the pull, Madria was standing beside him. *She must have lightning fast reflexes.*

"I want to go to the garden with you." She slipped the tunic on and belted it.

He raised his eyebrows at her curiously. "Good guess…and of course you can come. I'd love the company." Madria's ability to second-guess his actions was uncanny. In fact, it was downright spooky. He thrust off the superstitious feeling that crawled up his back, causing a shiver to pass over his backbone.

Opening the door, he searched the woods with his eyes. "Kitty, kitty, kitty," he called loudly then sighed. What had happened to his sweet feline companion? He noticed that Madria gave him a sad look.

She became invigorated once they stepped outside. The morning air was cool and refreshing. He whistled on the way and she clapped her hands.

"I love it when you whistle that tune."

"What?" He stopped dead in his tracks and stared at her.

She sidled up to him and rubbed against his body. "I meant, I love to hear that tune whistled."

"Oh." Antonius shook his head at himself. He had to remember Madria was not from around here—perhaps the language gave her difficulties at times. He waved toward the woods. "I, ah, need to go off for a minute."

"Me too."

They met at the same place a few minutes later. Madria had a strange look on her face. Continuing with the walk, they soon reached the stone fence. "Do you remember anything Madria...like where you are from?"

She shook her head, her eyes wary.

Antonius thought she did remember more than she was willing to share. All right then, he could be patient. "You can tell me, when you're ready." She stared back at him and gave a slight nod.

When he approached a row of wheat plants, a rabbit hopped from beneath it and ran across the field. He heard Madria's heavy breathing. Turning, he saw she seemed agitated. Her eyes shone and were glued to the rabbit's disappearing body, while her legs trembled.

"That rabbit didn't frighten you, did it?" He turned her toward him. She had that wild look on her face. *Was she really frightened of a tiny rabbit, or was it something else?*

"Yes...no...I don't know." She gazed down as if in confusion.

"Come, you can help me weed." He showed Madria which plants to work on. Glancing up a few minutes later, he was shocked to see her pull the pea plant up, roots and all. Several more lay by her side. *More bizarre behavior.*

"Not the chick peas." His voice shot out firmly and she crouched down, her eyes worried. Antonius sighed. Clearly she'd never done farming work before. More evidence of being from a wealthy family.

"Do you wish to help me?" He kept his tone soft.

"It's boring…and dirty." She stared at the weed in his hand, a moue of distaste on her face.

"You're right. Something a lady shouldn't have to do." He waved a hand toward the fence. "Why don't you just sit and watch." He wasn't too sure she should be working anyway.

She nodded and strolled away. Once reaching the fence, she stretched her body along the top, plopping her head on top of her hands. The fence was narrow even for her slim body, but she appeared to have good balance.

A shiver ran down his back. It was eerie how similar to his cat she looked. Madria had lain for hours just so, watching him work while she lazed atop the fence. Shaking his head at the silly thoughts that kept flying into it, Antonius went to work. Approximately an hour later, he glanced up. Madria was sound asleep. It was a wonder she hadn't rolled off the stone, but she seemed comfortable on her perch.

As if sensing his perusal, she glanced up. Madria watched him for a time, then strolled off. She was gone for a long time, perhaps taking a walk in the woods. He shouldn't worry—she was a big girl.

It was getting hot and almost lunchtime when he was satisfied that all his plants were weed free. Grabbing the water gourd and bag containing food, he headed for the large cypress tree where Madria was asleep beneath its shade. After taking a long drink from the gourd, he pulled out cheese and bread.

"More of the same?" Madria had sat up, her disapproving look stating what she thought of his lunch.

"You seem to be used to much better table fare." Antonius watched her reaction carefully for clues.

Shrugging delicately, she said, "Perhaps... I seem to remember more meat."

Ah. The signals were pointing more and more toward wealth. "Come, share my simple offering."

She laughed and resettled herself next to him. After they started eating, she seemed happy enough, even licking the cheese oil off her fingers as she'd done early that morning.

When they finished, she sat with her back propped against the tree. "Rest for a while." Patting the ground, she waited for him to stretch out beside her. Relaxing on a nice grassy spot, he wasn't surprised when Madria slipped down and cuddled next to him. She loved to snuggle.

He awoke with a raging hard-on. One of Madria's hands was sliding up and down his cock, while she licked his neck.

"Mmm, salty."

"Madria." He tried to push her away, but she wouldn't budge. "I'm all sweaty."

"I know," she purred. "I like the taste."

His engorged flesh jerked at her words.

"He likes the idea too," she whispered into his ear as she squeezed him gently.

Her tongue swiped around his ear, then she blew on the wetness and he shivered. Her mouth moved around to his and he tasted cheese. Their tongues danced in movements as old as the gods. Madria's tongue excited him with her demanding strokes.

Moving from his lips, she nibbled down his neck. Antonius' breathing deepened when her tongue laved his throat. Never had he been kissed on the neck. The sensation was erotic and burning hot.

He stroked Madria's hair, kneading her scalp unconsciously as she licked her way to his chest. When her warm, rather rough tongue laved one nipple, his whole body jumped.

"Mercy."

Chapter Five

Soft hair flowed over his torso, exciting him further. His balls were so tight they felt on the verge of exploding. Looking down, he couldn't see with all that hair covering his torso, where Madria's mouth was. But he could feel. Wet, hot lips caressed his stomach, then the tip of his cock was enveloped by her mouth.

He groaned and shoved his hips upward. Her mouth released him and that wonderful tongue stroked all the way from the tip to the base of his shaft.

"Madria," he moaned as her tongue laved one ball. She licked the other, then sucked each in turn into her hot cavern.

Her mouth returned to his cock, taking his whole member inside. Antonius panted and pushed her head toward his groin. His cock moved up and down in a fucking motion as he imagined ramming into her slick pussy. The soft slide of her full lips against his hard flesh was exciting, pushing him close to an orgasm. He felt fluid leak from the head of his cock, but maintained control, just barely.

Plopping him out, she flicked the head. "Mmmm, you taste delicious."

He glanced down at her lovely face. Her hair was wild and spread over his lower body. His cock was just below her chin, and as he watched, she stretched out that long tongue and gave it another lick.

A groan was ripped from him. He couldn't take his eyes off her. He should stop Madria if he wanted to make love to her, but Antonius couldn't do anything except stare at her actions.

Switching positions slightly, she gripped his cock with one hand and continued to watch his face. Now he could see everything she did to him. His staff disappeared as her mouth slipped over it. He jerked and almost came, but with a mammoth effort, he maintained control.

Releasing his swollen flesh, she gave it a quick kiss. That long, pink tongue snaked out, flicking the head, making his whole cock throb. Then her tongue slid around the shaft, almost going around the circumference—he was amazed at the flexibility.

But the sensation of having a hot, wet tongue sliding back and forth around his cock was too much. His hands tangled in her hair as an orgasm gripped his guts and tightened his balls almost painfully. His seed shot out and he moaned as he watched Madria.

Her tongue flicked out, lapping up droplets that flowed down his skin. His hips pumped as the last of his cum spurted out, and Madria licked up every drop.

After they cuddled for a while, she jumped up. She had a restless look on her face.

"I want to walk in the woods."

"All right," he laughed. "I guess I can stop work for today." His garden was doing well. A day of playing with her would be fun.

Redressing, they both headed for his favorite trail. He was surprised—it was as if Madria knew where it was. He shrugged. Antonius realized she must have seen the opening in the bushes.

They walked for hours. Neither talked much, spending most of their time observing nature around them. Madria seemed excited every time they spied a bird, rabbit, or any woodland creatures. *She must love animals.*

All along the way, he called for Madria, his cat, but she didn't show. Finally, he headed for his favorite spot—the river. Once they arrived, he sat under a large oak for a long time, pitching tiny rocks into the water. Madria sat next to him, but her attention strayed frequently to the rustling movements in the bushes surrounding them.

His thoughts kept returning to the strange, wondrous woman by his side. Who was she? Where did she come from? Was she human or something else?

Out of the corner of his eye, he saw her shaking her hands, trying to dislodge the dirt clinging to them. She'd been sitting propped up, but now seemed disturbed by the earth spotting her hands.

Even though he'd seen her lick her fingers clean before, it still surprised Antonius when she started licking the dirt off. Not wanting to be rude, he watched her from his side vision. After a short while she seemed to be satisfied with her fingers.

Then she flicked at the dirt scattered on her legs. A frown of distaste pulled at her lips. Bending down, she licked one lower leg.

A frisson of astonishment ran through him. This was beyond strange — it was running into bizarre. He didn't realize her behavior could become even more odd. She raised that leg, until it was straight up. He was amazed at her dexterous move and shocked when she began to lick the flesh of her upper thigh. His cock sprang to life at her actions.

She made a frustrated sound and he realized she was trying to go higher on her thigh, but couldn't.

Easing her leg back down, she stared around angrily. "I can't clean myself properly." Her nails dug into her legs, as she moved her hands up her thighs, leaving welts. "I'm dirty."

Antonius swallowed hard. He didn't want to really contemplate what her behavior meant, for it would be too unsettling. No matter how he tried to rationalize her actions, none seemed truly logical, at least for a human. Nonhuman then? That thought caused a ripple of unquiet in his heart. If she were not human that meant she was something else. And surely a mystical being wouldn't choose to stay with him long-term. Perhaps he was but a mere dalliance, a plaything for a short time.

Thrusting his disturbing thoughts aside, he chose distraction. "I know what to do." With that statement, he jumped up and held out one hand.

Madria gave him a puzzled look, but took his hand. Once he reached the river's edge, she refused to budge, stiffening her legs against his tug.

"What are you doing?"

"Going to take a bath," he chuckled. Thinking Madria may not favor the coolness of the water he decided to help her get over her trepidation quickly. Grabbing her by the waist, he moved backwards, pulling her into the water with him.

Flailing arms hit him in the face and chest, while her legs banged against his. A loud screeching hurt his ears. Intent on following through, Antonius secured her arms with some difficulty, and then fell backwards until the water covered them both.

After coming up for air, Madria screamed loudly. It was a very frightened sound. Releasing her swiftly, he was surprised at the speed in which she ran from the water.

She stood shivering on the riverbank. The long locks covered her face, but then she flipped them back. She was fuming, her eyes staring at him as if she'd like to bite his head off.

"It's not that cold." He held a laugh inside.

"It is…water," she hissed. Her teeth chattered and her body shook.

Antonius sighed and walked out. Madria backed away quickly.

"You're that angry about a dip in the river?"

Her furious stare answered for her. Shaking his head, he sat down and propped his back against a tree. The sun shone hotly upon his body. He would dry in no time. Madria picked a spot some dozen feet away and huddled on the ground, her face turned up to the sun. She looked miserable.

Chapter Six

Madria didn't know if she would ever understand humans. She remembered Antonius had the strange ritual of splashing in the river. But he had never attempted to throw her in when she was a cat. She had been shocked and terrified when he pulled her into the liquid.

While she huddled under the hot sun and dried, her thoughts flitted back over yesterday. She'd just finished eating a field mouse when the thunderstorm had burst overhead. Running beneath a thick bush, she had shivered while waiting for it to pass.

Two gods had materialized in the clearing in front of her. Madria knew them to be gods because she had seen a few before, but had always managed to run away. The humans worshiped these beings, but the animals simply ran from them in fear. The gods were common knowledge among the animal kingdom, and were to be avoided.

Mothers taught their offspring the signs to distinguish gods from humans. Gods shone so brightly, it hurt your eyes if you stared at them. These beings also spoke all languages, including animal. It was most disconcerting to hear the words in your head.

Madria had never been near enough to *hear* the gods before. But as she huddled beneath that dripping bush, she heard the two arguing. None of it made sense to her, but she still listened, fascinated in spite of her fear.

One of the beings, the male, threw a lightning bolt. The whole area was lit brilliantly. Madria hissed. She would have run, but her limbs were paralyzed with terror.

Both gods turned and saw her. The muscles in her legs continued to disobey her command to run, so she crouched there like a plump pigeon as they approached. They argued a bit more, but Madria was too terrified to follow the flow of words through her mind.

The female god pointed toward her. Madria's whole body screamed with pain and she became disoriented. When her vision cleared, the gods were gone and she found to her dismay, she'd been changed into a human female. This was the reason mothers warned their children to stay away from the gods and their tricks.

Only one thought had been in her muddled mind after that—safety. She had dragged herself home and managed to scratch on the door before passing out.

Ever since she had woken as a human, things had been very confusing. Speech had been in her mind from the beginning, so she could actually converse with her master. When still a cat, she'd understood a few words Antonius said to her, but mostly she went by feeling. Now that she truly could understand him, it was a wondrous thing, but also very frightening.

How long did the gods intend on playing this game? Madria didn't know, but had decided to be as human as she could while it lasted. Her former cat memories interfered quite often. Antonius' idea of a bath had infuriated and scared her.

After they both dried off, Antonius suggested they return home. She hit at a branch in the path with her human hands, then held them in front of her face. They really were very handy for doing things. Hands were something she would miss when she returned to her cat body. She touched her head. She would also miss her understanding of words.

Watching her master walk in front of her, she admired his calves. Never before had she realized he had a nice physique for a human. The long, hard thing between his legs, humans called a cock, fascinated her. Just thinking of it made the area between her legs warm.

It was strange, but she had been physically drawn to Antonius immediately after waking, and this had continued. It was as if she were in heat all the time. Madria sighed. The hot sex between them was priceless. This she would miss the most.

The thought of returning to her cat form made her feel funny inside. Something tickled her face and Madria swiped that area with her fingers. Water drenched her fingertips. She frowned. Water? On her face? She sniffed it—no smell. Human senses were pitiful compared to her cat ones. Sticking her tongue out, she licked it. Salty.

Madria searched her faint cat memories and suddenly knew the answer. She had seen Antonius with water running down his face when a dear friend of his had died last year. Now she remembered the word—tears or crying. The knowledge came with that word. Crying usually occurred when humans felt sad.

Was she sad? Not now. She kicked a stone in the trail. Sadness had gripped her when she thought of returning to her cat body. But that wasn't right, she longed for that, or at least part of her did. The sorrow returned as she realized it was the thought of leaving Antonius and the relationship that had developed between them, which had set off this strange feeling.

She had loved her master even while a cat. But what they had between them now would no longer be once she returned to her cat form. Another trickle of wetness hit her face and she wiped it away angrily. She had no say over the matter—it was all up to the gods.

When they reached the cottage, Madria was determined to get clean. She sniffed her arm and wrinkled her nose. River water smell. It was frustrating that she couldn't clean herself by licking anymore. That had been so simple.

Madria frowned as she recalled the first time she'd used the bathroom as a human. Now that had been a horrible situation, trying to figure everything out. The worst problem had been how to clean her bottom. Luckily she remembered seeing Antonius a few times when they were in the woods. At the time, she had thought his using leaves was silly, but it worked when she tried it.

She was shaken from her musings as Antonius moved across her vision, walking to the well. He drew a bucket of water, sipped on it then held it out toward her. Drinking from the clay ladle, she had a sudden remembrance.

After he returned from working in the fields, Antonius would pour a bucket of water into a large bowl. Then using a cloth, he rubbed it all over his body. He used a piece of…the word soap popped in her mind…to cleanse the dirt from him. She much preferred his sweaty odor, but his smell after he took a bath, was nice in a different way.

"I want to wash up. Can I borrow your soap?"

Antonius nodded, and then strode quickly into the house, returning with a sliver of soap and a small cloth. Madria had brought the bowl, which he kept on a table near the door, to the well.

Taking the items from him, she laid them on the well's stone, then slipped off the tunic. Handing the apparel to Antonius, she was gratified by the gleam of lust that flamed in his eyes. Holding back a shudder, she dipped the cloth into the water and squeezed it out as she remembered her master doing.

Using the soap, she washed then rinsed her body with the water. About halfway through the procedure, Madria realized something surprising. The water didn't feel bad like it did the time she had slipped into the water as a cat while crossing over some rocks. She ran one finger along the skin on her arm. She no longer had long fur, and the water didn't make her human hair feel matted or nasty. Actually, it felt rather pleasant.

After she finished, Antonius threw a bucket of water over his body and then soaped it. Even his hair was soaked, making the light brown locks look black. He looked quite funny with white bubbles spotting his skin. A strange sensation erupted from inside her. Madria made a most bizarre sound. It took a few seconds for the word to come to her—giggling. As she watched her master rinse off, Madria decided she liked this human giggle. It left her with a good feeling inside.

She also decided Antonius looked too good to leave alone. His muscles stood out in bold relief with the water dripping down his tanned flesh. She licked her lips, suddenly wondering what watery human skin would taste like.

Stepping up to him, she took his cock in one hand and circled her other arm behind his neck, pulling him down for a kiss. The mumbling protests beneath her lips quieted in a few seconds as her hand stroked his cock into hardness.

Releasing his lips, she nibbled her way down his body, dipping her tongue into his navel then continuing. Antonius groaned and put his hands in her hair when her tongue slid over the tip of his staff.

He pulled her upward after she sucked on his cock a short while. "Your turn."

His eyes told her he had something delicious in mind, and she shivered in anticipation.

Chapter Seven

"Wait here." Antonius ran into the house and returned quickly with a large lambskin throw. He spread it beneath the huge oak tree.

Reaching the throw swiftly, she knelt, dug her fingers into the soft wool, and then glanced up at her master. His eyes washed over her body and he rubbed his chin.

Madria faced forward, waiting impatiently for his cock to slip inside her already moist flesh. Her breath hitched as his hands grazed the soft skin of her butt. When he kneaded each globe, she couldn't help but push backwards into his hands.

Next, his lips placed warm kisses to each cheek. She arched her back. When his hot tongue slid between the wetness of her lower lips, she meowed and her head flopped weakly to the cushiony throw.

His tongue wiggled deeper, slipping into her channel. She moaned and pushed back, sheathing his tongue even more in her flesh. That marvelous tongue seemed to fill her. It slid in and out, just as his cock did when he used it.

Madria scratched the wooly throw beneath her and dug her nails into its softness. His tongue slipped out and stroked the center of her pleasure—that which humans called a clit. That tiny piece of flesh throbbed with the blood pounding through it.

She moaned loudly as his tongue flicked the nub. Rubbing her face into the throw, she panted. It was too much—this wild, fierce heat that ripped through her clit.

A loud scream erupted from her as her pussy convulsed. Her scream ended in a screeching yowl. Antonius kept licking at her hot flesh until her body went limp.

Breathing heavily, she awaited his next move. Satisfaction flashed through her when the large head of his cock nudged her opening. Spreading her legs wider, she held her breath as he slipped slowly inside.

"Yes," she whispered.

It was enough to encourage her master. His thrusts became deeper and harder.

"Yes," she screamed this time. "Do it harder." She rammed her wet flesh onto his engorged cock.

Her butt jiggled as Antonius plunged into her repeatedly. His staff swelled larger and her vagina clamped tighter around it in reaction.

Madria moaned as his seed gushed into her. Her inner walls responded with tiny shudders.

She was so relaxed after they finished, she stretched out on the lambskin. Antonius lay down beside her, staring up at the leaves overhead. It was shady beneath the oak and a light wind made it very pleasant. Drifting off to sleep took no effort.

Waking to hunger pains, she glanced over at her master. He was still napping. Running one hand up his nearer thigh woke him instantly.

"I'm hungry," she stated flatly when he turned toward her.

Sitting up, he ran a hand through his hair. "I'll catch our fish dinner." He stood and smiled at her. "I don't suppose you want to come with me?"

Shaking her head, she yawned. "I'll stay here."

Madria was startled awake again by a nudge to her arm. Blinking sleepily, she stared up at Antonius. Her nose detected a new odor. Fish! Her mouth watered when she spied the string of fish he held.

Antonius took the catch to the table by the door, gutted them, and then scraped the scales off. She swallowed the salvia pooling in her mouth.

Leaping to her feet, she grabbed one of the fish and bit into it. Ignoring Antonius' astonished look, she chewed. Nasty. Spitting the meat from her mouth, she stared at the fish. Why did it taste horrible? This had never happened before.

Handing the bass back to her master, she watched him stick the fish on a stick and place it over the outside cooking pit. She spit again and rubbed her mouth. It must be the human side of her. She remembered that Antonius always ate his fish cooked. Sighing, she sat down across from him. She'd just have to wait.

Bringing two clay plates, her master plunked a fish on each plate when they were done, and handed her one.

"It's still hot," he warned as she started to take a pinch.

Madria's mouth watered again. The fish smelled delicious.

Antonius picked up a charred stick from the fire and poked at the meat. It fell into little chunks. Glancing at her, he said, "It'll cool faster."

Grabbing a stick, she broke her fish into pieces. When it cooled enough to take a bite, Madria closed her eyes in ecstasy. Nothing had ever tasted so good.

It didn't take too long for them to eat all six fish. Lounging back afterwards, she felt very content.

They spent the rest of the evening sprawled on the lamb throw, which Antonius had moved to an area clear of overhanging branches. As they gazed up at the many stars, he pointed out constellations and named gods or goddesses associated with each. Madria shivered. Gods were tricksters.

Glancing at Antonius, she realized she should be grateful to the gods. If not for those two that day, she wouldn't have been able to experience a physical relationship with her master. That thought made sadness flush through her, for surely it couldn't last. Madria turned her attention back to Antonius' words. His tale about one of the gods did manage to distract her.

* * * * *

Jupiter gazed down at the cat maiden. He was worried about the bet he had with the lovely Venus. Although Madria had adjusted well to her human form and every day she seemed to act less like a cat, he still wasn't sure of the outcome. He had to win the bet. A chance to spend a torrid night in Venus' arms wouldn't come again. That was if he won. Jupiter smiled to himself. Many humans thought Venus was his daughter, but she wasn't. Making love to the sexy goddess was one of his most vivid wishes that had not yet been fulfilled.

If he lost, he'd promised to give Venus a flying horse to pull her new chariot. Catching a creature like Pegasus was very difficult, even for a god. Besides, he loved to watch the horses flying and galloping in freedom. But he'd made the wager. Winning was the only option he acknowledged.

Watching the cat girl stroll restlessly through the woods, Jupiter got an idea. If he could push her human emotions more, then maybe she would soon forget her cat origins. The more he thought about it, the more he was intrigued by the possibilities. Madria was a lovely human and he wouldn't mind sampling her charms while pursuing his goal of igniting her human emotions.

Chapter Eight

Madria took a long walk in the woods. It was another day and Antonius was working in his garden, but she quickly got bored watching him work. She was restless. As she walked, her mind spiraled round and round her dilemma. Was she human or cat?

Coming into a beautiful little clearing surrounded on all sides by thick bushes, she paused to look around. Before, she would have been checking the undergrowth for mice or lizards. Now, she contemplated the serene loveliness of the setting. Being human certainly had changed her view on many matters.

A rustling noise drew her eyes to the far side of the clearing. A young human male stepped forward, smiling at her. By human standards, he was very handsome. His sculpted face with its square jaw and high cheekbones could have been carved by an artist. She smiled at that thought. Her master could do justice to such a face.

Although Antonius' face was not as strongly formed, she liked it better. Her master had a very "human" face, one in which his sensitive artistic nature was very evident. The stranger's face was almost too perfect.

Her eyes ran down his form. His biceps bulged and a hint of his muscular chest could be seen below the neckline of the tunic. Madria was quite sure the rest of his body would match his face and the parts she could see.

"Who are you?" she asked idly, not really caring, but she had found that polite conversation was a part of human etiquette.

"A stranger." He walked slowly toward her.

"If you wish to enjoy the beauty of this spot alone," she waved her hand. "I was about to leave anyway."

"But then you will be taking the greatest part of the beauty with you." He grinned, transforming his face into even more male handsomeness.

Madria didn't know what to make of the stranger and his remark. Some part of her was pleased at his words, but part was uncomfortable.

The man walked to within arms length of her. "I saw you and I knew immediately I must have you."

"Have me?" She knew her eyes flashed fire. His remark made her angry. Presumptuous. Like the male toms who took any female they could and made them submit to them.

Another charming smile marked his face. "Perhaps I phrased that a bit roughly. I meant that I would love to get better acquainted."

"How?" She was being purposely obstinate.

"Perhaps this way." He stepped forward and placed his arms around her.

Madria knew he meant making love in spite of his clever words. She was on the point of scratching his face, but then curiosity got the better of her. Antonius was the only male she'd been with while in human form. Sex was a wondrous journey each time they set upon it. Would another male's kisses be different? Would it be as wonderful?

He must have seen something in her eyes, for his face descended slowly toward her. When his soft lips latched onto hers, she returned his kiss with no qualms. His tongue urged her to open and she did. The dance of their tongues was most pleasant, but she instantly realized it did not compare to the heat between her and Antonius.

Not one to give up easily in new explorations, Madria allowed the man to kiss her for long minutes. His hand slipped her tunic down on the left side and he caressed her breast. Warm rushes of excitement ran through her skin where he touched. Nice, but again, nothing like her master elicited from her.

His head moved down her throat, and then she felt his warm tongue lave her breast. Pleasant. But abruptly a strange sensation shot through her nerves. Invasion. She didn't know where that word came from, but she knew the meaning. This man was exploring her body in ways that she realized she did not want. Only one man should be allowed such liberties.

Pushing him back, she readjusted her tunic. "That was nice, but it is enough."

"Enough!" His voice rose. "We just got started."

"I don't want you," she mimicked his earlier words. "I just wanted to see if your kisses stirred me as much as another."

"And have they?" he demanded.

She shrugged. "As I said, nice, but no, not anywhere near what I experience with Antonius."

"You tease a man then leave him hot and horny?"

"It was not meant that way. I was curious."

He stared at her, his look going thoughtful, as if he just realized something. "This Antonius is a lucky man."

Those words made her happy. Without another word, the man turned and strode back through the bushes. Madria decided to wait a bit before leaving. She did not want to run into him again. Now that the incident was over, she knew she had been pushing dangerous ground in this human realm of emotions.

After ten minutes of contemplating the beauty of the clearing, she started back the way she came—opposite of the direction the man had disappeared into the bushes. A sudden wind whipped through the open area, making her tunic flap madly. Glancing up at the sky, she was surprised at the brilliant blue. No storm clouds in sight.

The wind increased as she took a step, and a gust picked her up, ramming her back into a large oak. She was stuck against the trunk, her heels kicking into the bark ineffectively. A tickling sensation drew her eyes to her wrists. Madria hissed in terror. Trailing vines were wrapping around her wrists even as she watched.

Tugging hard, she couldn't dislodge the things. Once wrapped several times around her wrists, the vines moved upward. Madria trembled as she watched her arms being pulled up. She was bound.

Movement around her legs made her look down fearfully. Ground creepers flowed around her ankles in spite of her fierce kicks. Once secured, the vines started crawling in different directions, so that her legs were splayed out. Queasiness gripped her stomach. This had to be more tricks of the gods.

Madria glanced up quickly, back to where the young man had disappeared. Was he a god disguised as a human? He had seemed too beautiful. She shivered violently, expecting him to emerge any second from the bushes.

The wind settled down except for a pleasant breeze. Movement on either shoulder made her go stiff with fright. The short sleeves were shoved down, until the material ripped, and then her breasts were bared as the tunic slid down. Madria's heart pounded and she found it hard to breathe as the dress was pushed down around her hips by something invisible.

The tunic could go no further, and whatever was removing her clothing seemed to realize it. A few seconds ticked by. She trembled all over. Unexpectedly the linen was torn from the neckline to the bottom. It fell in a heap at the base of the tree.

Madria swallowed and squeaked out, "Who is there?"

Only the wind answered, by lifting her hair, as if teasing her.

She tugged against the vines, struggling to get free of this magical confinement. The wind gusted again, blowing against her body. It flowed across her breasts, causing them to peak, making them move as if a lover stroked them.

Madria bit her bottom lip. She was terrified and felt like she could throw up any minute. But at the same time, the windy caresses made her breasts tingle. Little gusts of wind stroked her body, moving from her breasts, down her legs, and tickling her abdomen.

Then the hair over her mons was ruffled. Holding her breath, she dared a look down. Nothing. But she could see and feel the wind blowing in warm puffs between her legs. As if finding its direction, the wind shot between her lower lips, stirring her senses with its gentle touch.

She moaned and closed her eyes. It wasn't fair. Her body was being invaded by an invisible lover, and she couldn't stop her sensitive body from reacting to the caressing touches of wind.

A clap of lightning startled her. She opened her eyes and stared around. Still no storm clouds. But then a tiny bolt of lightning appeared six feet in front of her, before it fizzled out. Madria panted in fear. The gods were having too much fun playing one of their games with her. She was getting angry.

"Stop it!" she shouted.

Was it her imagination that she heard a soft chuckle?

Chapter Nine

The wind picked up again and attacked all her sensitive parts at once. It squeezed her breasts and flicked her nipples with tiny blows, while gusts slipped between her pussy lips.

"No," she groaned, grinding her head against the bark. She didn't want to respond to this intrusive power.

The lightning bolt struck again and she watched with terror-stricken eyes as tiny charges went off in front of her body. Then two bolts sizzled right in front of each nipple. Madria tried to shrink backward into the trunk, but it didn't help. The minute lightning struck each pebbled nub. Zap! Zap! Over and over, the electric-charged things hit her nipples.

Madria shuddered as shards of pleasure lanced through her torso. She moaned and arched her back, thrusting her breasts toward the pleasure givers. While the tiny bolts continued their sensual attack, she felt the sizzle of air stir between her legs. Daring to look down, she was panting with fear and excitement when she saw several swirling bolts dancing directly in front of her pussy.

Suddenly, as if in coordination, the bolts shot out, one after another and hit her clit. At the same time, the lightning on her nipples continued their electric strokes. She moaned loudly and her legs flopped loosely. Without being aware of it, her hips shoved forward and her legs opened wider.

"Yes," she whimpered, grinding her head against the trunk.

As if responding to her excitement, the tiny bolts struck her nipples and clit faster and harder. It didn't hurt, but set off such a deep, aching desire throughout her whole body, until she felt as if her heart would pound out of her chest.

"Yes!" she screamed long and loud. Her pussy convulsed with one strong orgasm after another. The bolts of lightning had softened, then petered out to nothing as her body went limp.

Madria hung, supported only by the vines holding her. Never had she experienced such a mind-blowing climax. But neither had she felt so violated. Her senses were aroused by an invisible lover. She could call it nature by virtue of the wind and bolts of lightning, but knew in reality it had to be a god calling the shots.

After she could catch her breath and some strength flowed into her body, she glanced up. No young man. No god shining with the sun's glow. Who had perpetrated this vile act on her? Frustrated and angry, Madria tugged against the vines. It did no good—they might as well have been chains. Someone wasn't through playing with her yet.

Jupiter would have rubbed his hands with glee, except he was invisible. The cat girl had responded much better than he could have anticipated. Of course, he had been frustrated with her when she refused his advances while he was in human form. But not one to be easily dissuaded, he had used wind and tiny bolts of lightning to excite her. His invisible hands had never touched her; he used them only to direct the elements of nature. It aroused him mightily to see her go wild with desire.

Now it was his turn. He wanted satisfaction. Madria was stirred to a fever-pitch of burning need. Would she be able to resist Antonius?

Madria turned her head swiftly when she heard a footstep. Antonius was walking toward her. Water gathered in her eyes. "Antonius! I'm so glad to see you."

He stopped just in front of her, his eyes flicking over her body. His eyes were molten with desire for her. She licked her lower lip and her clit throbbed. It was surprising to her that she wanted him so badly after what she had just been through. But there it was, and she had never denied her feelings as a cat or as a woman.

Another surprise was that her master didn't act upset at finding her bound to a tree. In fact, his dark brown eyes told her that it ignited his desire. Maybe tying their lovers up was a part of human sexuality she had not been privy to before. She shrugged inside. Whatever the strange rites, she wanted to go along with this game.

He caught her head and brought her forward, latching onto her lips with a fierceness that sent a thrill through her. She whimpered as his tongue stabbed at hers, while the other hand stroked her breasts.

Releasing her head and edging back a bit, both his hands caressed her breasts as he watched her face.

"Does that feel good?"

"Yes, oh, yes," she moaned, shoving her nipples into his palms. She licked her lip. She wanted his mouth on her aching flesh.

As if reading her thoughts, his head descended to her left breast. She sighed when his hot mouth covered her nub, then groaned and arched her back when he sucked on it. The soft curls on his head brushed her breast, setting up new sensations in the sensitive skin.

Watching him suckle her flesh made her hotter. It felt like those bolts of lightning were still around, that they were crawling through her nerves, shooting sparks of desire into her nipples and pussy.

It was strange, but her being tied helplessly while Antonius loved her body was more exciting than she could have dreamed it would be. She was vulnerable and at his mercy, but it caused her to feel red-hot in all the sensitive areas of her body. She wanted his hands to caress her flesh while she twisted against the vines. Wanted him to fuck her as she lay spread-legged and bound.

"Yes, my love, do with me as you will." Madria couldn't seem to stop the words from escaping. Words that gave him complete power over her. Over her will as well as her body.

Antonius' head came back up and he captured her mouth in a forceful kiss while he pressed his body into her—hard. She felt his cock nudging her, then grinding against her mons. She had no idea when he undressed and didn't care at this point.

"You desire me to ram my cock inside you?"

His voice was rough. Never had she heard Antonius speak so coarsely. It excited her to a higher level.

"Yes," she whispered.

Holding her waist, he pulled her down slightly, adjusting his cock at her entrance. She was surprised the vines gave at all, as they seemed to resist when she pulled against them. He thrust into her with one stroke. Madria groaned loudly and gripped the vines hanging above her wrists.

His cock seemed huge, filling her to the point that it almost hurt. His body ground into her as he rammed his hard flesh inside her over and over.

"Mmm," she whimpered, her nails digging into the stiff vines.

"You like being fucked?" He plunged forcefully inside as he asked his question.

She nodded.

"Tell me." He demanded her response, his cock thrusting into her with such power, her lower body bounced at each stroke.

"Fuck me, Antonius," she moaned, staring into his hot gaze.

She didn't think he could enter her with more force, but he did. Her body shook from his power.

His hands touched her ankles and she felt the vines fall away. Then he pulled her knees up and splayed them wide. On some far away level she was confused by his ability to so easily loosen the vines that she had struggled against. But he was setting her body on fire so that thoughts flew out of her mind.

In this new position, she was more vulnerable and open. He slammed his cock into her slick flesh, pulling a whimper from her. His cock head hit her womb and hurt a bit, but pleasure ignited even more fiercely, overriding the pain.

He withdrew and held his cock at her opening, teasing it with soft strokes.

"What do you want, pussy?" His voice was deep and filled with husky desire.

She whimpered and tried to shove herself back down upon him. But he withheld his staff so that she was unable to do so.

"Your cock," she said fiercely. When he eased back inside her, she panted, shoving her inner walls around him. "Yes!" As he took up his powerful strokes again, her whole body seemed to go into orgasm. She shook with the force of her climax, and her vagina spasmed around his cock.

"Such a hot pussy," Antonius screamed, ramming to the hilt inside her.

She clutched at his cock as his seed burst inside her sensitive walls, milking his stiff flesh until he stopped all movement. Her lower lips throbbed and she moaned when he moved slightly, his still engorged staff exciting her once again.

Unexpectedly, he turned his head, listening. Withdrawing without another word, he grinned at her, then started walking away.

"Wait, aren't you going to untie me?"

He turned, still smiling. "Yes, I will in a moment."

That was the most bizarre statement he'd ever made. Madria was aggravated. How could he leave her bound like this, even for a moment? He pushed through the greenery, disappearing completely.

Mere seconds later she heard the bushes rustle and watched as he stepped through and glanced around the clearing. When his eyes lit on her, his mouth fell open. He acted like he had not seen her before. Antonius jogged up to her and started tugging at the vines binding her wrists.

"Madria, what happened?"

Chapter Ten

A sour taste rose in her mouth. She suddenly knew what had happened to her. She had been seduced by a god. He had disguised himself as Antonius, for otherwise she would not have consented to have sex with him. She flopped in her master's arms after he untied her. It had to be the young man who first appeared to her. Being unsuccessful, he had wickedly bound her and played with her using his powers over nature. Finally, he had appeared as Antonius to fool her.

"Madria." He shook her shoulders gently.

She hid her face against his chest. She had to answer him, tell him something. "Some man tied me up and had his way with me."

"By the gods! Where did he go?"

"I don't know," she mumbled into his chest hair. "I fainted."

Antonius stroked her hair. "My poor Madria." He bent down and picked her up.

She tried to protest, but she really was awfully weak. It felt nice nestled in his arms. Water fell from her eyes. How she wished it had been her master who made love to her. He carried her for a long way, but finally he stopped to take a break.

"I can walk, if you help me."

He placed one of her arms around his waist and they walked slowly the last two miles. Once there, Antonius insisted that she rest in the bed. He went outside and returned with the bath bowl. Gently, he washed her face then carefully cleansed her wrists and ankles. He was being so kind she felt tears in her eyes again. Blinking them back forcefully, she watched Antonius wash her. There was no use upsetting him more than he already was.

"I should clean there." He waved the cloth at her groin.

She nodded. She did feel dirty.

Antonius was so gentle. His head was bent to his task, but when he raised it to look at her, she was shocked to see his eyes watering.

"It is all right." She caressed his cheek.

He clutched her hand in his. "It is I who should be doing the reassuring." He rearranged her cover, then kissed her forehead. "Rest."

Antonius grabbed his large staff he kept by the door on the way out. He usually carried it in case he ran into snakes. For some reason his action made her uneasy.

Madria fell asleep, waking only when she heard her master return. He had a frown on his face, and he didn't look happy. Sitting up, she asked, "Where did you go?"

He glanced at her, then propped the large stick against the wall. "To look for him." He came over and sat on the edge of the bed. "I'm sorry, I couldn't find any sign of him." Staring over her head, he frowned again. "Strange, I didn't even find any tracks."

"It's all right, it's over with."

"You keep trying to make me feel better, when I should be doing that for you." He sounded frustrated.

"Antonius, you have been showing me that you care." She shrugged. "It happened, it wasn't my fault, so I must put it behind me."

He stared at her, astonishment written across his expressive face. "I don't know how you can be so strong… I don't know that I can forget that easily."

Yawning, Madria thought up the quickest way to stop this discussion. "I'm tired." She snuggled under the covers, enjoying Antonius' attention as he fussed over her.

"I'm going to go get supper."

Nodding, she watched him leave. Was he really going after supper or going looking for that man again? She was determined to thrust the whole incident from her mind. After all, it was another game played on her by a god. What could she do? Be more careful when out in the woods, her mind whispered.

Madria snorted at her human thoughts. Silly. How could one prepare for the gods and their tricks? Right now, her main concern was seeing that what happened didn't affect the relationship between her and Antonius.

This time when she awoke, it was to a delicious odor. Fish. Jumping out of bed, Madria was surprised that her body did feel sore and abused. Slowing her pace, she headed outside.

"Mmm, you caught us fish."

"Should you be up?" He stood up quickly and took one of her arms.

"I'm fine." She let him guide her to a log to sit on. He was so sweet and considerate. This new protective behavior of his made her feel all warm inside.

The fish were done, and he put two large ones on a plate, handing it to her. Remembering his cooling technique, she broke the meat apart with a stick. After supper they talked about mundane things, the garden, and the new clay figure Antonius needed to start on. They both seemed to be tiptoeing around the subject foremost in their minds.

Madria was glad when it finally was bedtime. It was weary work, keeping her master from thinking about what had happened to her.

* * * * *

Over the next few days, she found that all Antonius thought about was the incident. At least, that's what his behavior indicated. He spent little time with his garden, and didn't even look at the clay which awaited his efforts. But he did spend hours rambling the woods.

He treated her with the kindness and thoughtfulness, even cooking her fish every night. Antonius knew how much she loved it. But he had not attempted to touch her in a sexual way. She watched as he came in that evening. His face was drawn. Many times, when he didn't think she was looking, his expression was filled with anger.

Finally, she knew what she must do. "Antonius." She had followed him back outside, where he was cleaning up. "We must talk."

His hand paused as he rubbed the cloth over his arm.

Walking up to him, she took the material and finished washing that arm. "You must give up on finding that man."

"Why?" His lips formed a flat line. Clearly he was displeased.

Placing the cloth on the well, she laid her hands softly on his face, turning it down to look at her. "Because it was a god."

"What?" His eyes were surprised. "How do you know?"

"Just trust me, I know." She shrugged. "There is little we mortals can do against gods' tricks."

"I know, but—"

She placed one finger against his lips, stilling his words. "One cannot fight a god…that is, if you could even find him." She smiled up at him.

Antonius stared at her, his expression pensive. Finally, he nodded.

Chapter Eleven

Several more days passed before Madria's temper took reign. She had been so pleased with Antonius' protective attitude and the caring way he looked after her. But enough was enough. She was not made of breakable clay like his creations. Now, she needed more than a gentle touch. She needed his hot hands on her body, letting her know how much he desired her.

Antonius returned to his farming duties. When he finished in the afternoon, he got the bowl ready for his bath.

"Here, let me do your back." Madria took the cloth from him. He had often asked her to scrub his back, but since the incident, he hadn't asked her to lift a finger.

Turning, Antonius stood stolidly while she rubbed the dirt from him. After she finished his back, her strokes continued down his legs. "Turn," she said softly.

He was stiff-faced when he turned to face her. Staying on her knees, she scrubbed the front of his legs. Occasionally, her fingers slipped off the material and caressed his bare skin. She was gratified to hear his breathing deepen. Thankfully, he was not immune to her touch.

His chest and arms had already been cleansed, leaving only his groin area. As her cloth-covered hand started trailing up toward his half-hard cock, he placed one hand over hers.

"You don't have to."

His whole body was tense, making his muscles stand out in bold relief. She knew Antonius fought to control his passion.

"But I want to," she whispered, gazing up at him. Dropping the cloth, she circled her hand around his now hard member. "Don't you want me anymore, Antonius?"

"By the gods, there is never a moment when I don't desire you," he said huskily.

"Then don't let anything come between us." She stood up and awaited his next move.

His face softened at her words and he pulled her gently into his arms.

Antonius was in agony when Madria wiped his back and legs. He'd longed for her touch, but didn't dare approach her. It seemed a callous attitude to wish for sex when she'd been through such a trauma only recently. Try as he might, he couldn't keep his cock from responding to her strokes, especially when she started doing his front side.

After her sad entreaty, he could not deny her, and was tired of denying himself. He was pleased with how eagerly she came into his arms. Their kiss was soft and sweet to start with, but quickly turned to one filled with hunger.

Picking her up, he carried Madria to the bed.

"So, you still want me?" She stared up at him, her look unsure.

He felt like an idiot. His attempt at kindness, by staying away from her, had led to her wondering if he no longer desired her.

"Yes." Antonius stroked her cheek and kissed her gently. "I am going to show you how much I want you." Running his hands through her hair, he massaged her head softly while they kissed. He wanted her to feel needed, but at the same time cherished by his gentle approach.

He spent much longer than normal applying light pressure to her lips and not demanding entrance with his tongue. Moving his lips slowly back and forth, he stretched out the erotic play between their mouths. Taking her lower lip into his mouth, he sucked it softly. Madria moaned, clearly enjoying the gentler side of lovemaking they had not explored yet. In previous sessions before, their bodies always seemed too overheated and too anxious to come together. But this time, he was determined to show Madria the way he felt, by acting as if they had all the time in the world.

Slipping his tongue to the opening of her mouth, he stroked slowly, urging her to open wide. Her sweet breath slid inside his mouth as he moved his tongue into hers. Slowly, he caressed her tongue with his. His cock was rock-hard and he ached for her.

He wanted to kiss and caress her for hours, but knew such a wish was impossible. He couldn't hold out that long from making love to her. As his rough, work-hardened fingers skimmed over her skin, he marveled anew at its silky texture. Never would he tire of stroking its unique softness.

Kissing his way ever so slowly down, his lips joined his hands that were caressing one breast. Madria moaned as his tongue swiped across her swollen nipple, causing it to pucker.

"Your breasts are perfect—fit for a goddess," he whispered against her flesh.

"Oh, please, not a goddess." Her chuckle turned into a groan as his tongue swirled around the nub.

Taking her nipple into his mouth, Antonius sucked gently, enjoying the increased rate of her breathing. Knowing what she liked, he placed more pressure into the suckling, while his other hand played with her right breast.

"Yes."

Her sigh flashed through him, setting new fires in his blood. His tongue flicked the pebbled flesh as his fingers rolled the other nipple.

"Antonius." Her body arched upward as the husky plea left her lips.

Releasing her nipple, he licked and nibbled his way down her abdomen. When his tongue laved her navel, her skin quivered. He glanced upward and saw that she was watching him. She knew what he had in mind and her eyes were fiery with desire and need. His cock ached to be inside her, but first he wanted to pleasure her.

His lips moved down to her legs and he sucked skin from her inner thigh into his mouth. She moaned and opened her legs wider. Giving the skin a last lick, he skimmed his tongue over her slit without penetrating it. Her flesh was already slick with her excitement.

Slipping his tongue deeper, Antonius entered her folds, tasting her delicious womanly flesh. His tongue lapped over and over along the whole length of her labia.

Madria's thighs trembled and she panted. Withdrawing his tongue, he tried something different, stabbing his tongue in swift flicks into her soft folds. She moaned loudly.

Parting her outer lips gently, he made the stabbing movements upon her clit. Madria's body flinched and she whimpered.

Easing forward slightly, he laved her clit in one long stroke. It hardened beneath his caresses. Her hands had glided into his hair and moved restlessly.

At the same time he ran his tongue around the circumference of the nub, he slipped one finger into her vagina.

Her body jumped and his tongue lost its place. Stroking his finger in and out, he watched her face. Her eyes were closed, and her creamy skin flushed with blood.

Returning to her lovely pussy, he flicked her clit with his tongue, gauging the speed to match with the rhythm of his finger. Slow, long glides, interspersed with swift, short strokes.

Madria screamed, it sounding more like a yowl, and her hips shoved upward, surrounding his lips with her fragrant, wet flesh. Antonius continued licking her clit while several orgasms trembled through her pussy. Giving her pouting lips a last kiss, he eased up her body.

Her arms draped around his neck and she pulled him forward. Their lips met in a searing kiss.

"Mmm, that was very, very nice," she said huskily.

"Are you ready for more?"

"Always," she sighed and wiggled her hips, rubbing her mons against his engorged cock.

Madria bent her knees, giving him easy access. Latching onto her mouth again, he slid slowly inside her. Wet heat wrapped around him like a glove, and her slick juices coated his cock.

Little whimpering cries of pleasure escaped her mouth and he caught them with a kiss. His balls slapped into her flesh as he thrust deeply into her pussy. He placed his arms under her knees, a groan wrenching from him as he slid in even further, penetrating her deeply with each thrust.

Biting her bottom lip, she made tiny "mmm" sounds. Leaning down, he splayed her knees as he captured her mouth again in a demanding kiss. She moaned and her hips moved in conjunction with his strokes.

Her nails raked along his back, leaving welts he was sure. It was painful but still turned him on.

Antonius was surprised, but immensely pleased when he felt the shudders of her vagina. Not wishing to climax yet, he withdrew his cock and concentrated on kissing her delectable lips. After his blood cooled from boiling point, he eased back onto his knees.

"Turn over, my love."

Madria eagerly flipped over into a kneeling position. She loved making love this way.

Chapter Twelve

When he eased inside, Antonius groaned at the exquisite sensation of her pussy around his throbbing cock. It seemed as if her skin resisted for a second, holding him at bay, but then he pushed past tight entrance. His breathing deepened as he plunged in and out. She was so hot and small, it felt like she was a virgin.

Madria made a sound deep in her throat, something unintelligible, when he rammed all the way inside her. Her body responded to his every stroke, and she shoved her hips backward each time.

Gripping a cheek in each hand, he pulled her cute butt back and forth, increasing the contact between them. Her warm, wet flesh called to him like some mysterious seductive creature. He groaned, thrusting into her with force as his cock swelled.

"Madria," he bellowed as his seed shot into her hot flesh.

Her vagina convulsed around him, milking his cock until he stopped pumping into her. They both fell forward, exhausted. Antonius rolled to the side, taking her with him and spooning her into his body.

After they rested, Antonius was hit by an urge to work on the clay. Bringing it outside, he placed the worktable under the shade. Setting the clay on the table, he stared at the formless material.

Madria brought the lambskin throw and stretched out near him. Her presence gave him an inspiration. "Can I use you as a model?"

"Me?" Her voice and face lit with pleasure. She nodded happily.

"Would it bother you, if I did a nude?"

"No," she laughed and pulled the tunic off quickly. "How do you wish me to pose?"

"On your side, like you were before."

Madria stretched out on her side and propped up on one elbow.

Antonius turned the clay on its side and started. He worked for hours, concentrating on forming the outline of her figure.

"I'm getting tired."

He glanced up. Poor Madria. She had held that position a long while. After covering the clay, he washed his hands, then sat down next to her. She repositioned herself onto her stomach. Moving her hair aside, he massaged her shoulders.

"Mmm, that feels nice."

Kneading her whole back, he was not surprised when she drifted off to sleep in a few minutes. Stretching out beside her, he stared at the leaves overhead. Madria slept more than anyone he'd ever known. And come to think of it, she hadn't done any work at all since he found her either. She hadn't even offered to cook.

Antonius exhaled a breath. Surely she must be from a wealthy family. That thought made him sad. He had come to care deeply for this beautiful, strange woman. Probably when she tired of playing the pauper's life, she would return to her family.

Recalling her odd behaviors, he wondered if she would return to the woods instead. Maybe to some secret place where magical beings gathered to dance beneath a brilliant moon.

Unexpectedly, he realized no matter where she returned to, he would miss her horribly. He wanted her to stay with him. The more he mulled over his thoughts, the clearer things became.

He loved Madria. Glancing at her sleeping form, he followed that thought to a natural conclusion. Should he ask her to stay as his wife? Yes, his mind answered back. But first, he wanted to be sure she felt the same way. He was sure Madria liked him, but love? He wasn't too confident about that.

Reality shot through his dreamy thoughts. He needed a wife who would work by his side, not make more work for him. He took a deep breath and exhaled slowly. Maybe that would be a test of her love. If Madria was willing to forgo her rich beginnings and live a humble life, then maybe there was hope for them.

Antonius fell asleep listening to Madria's soft breathing. He was awakened by her hot kisses on his mouth and strokes to his hard cock. That was another thing he loved about her—Madria was so sexual and always eager to make love.

She giggled when she noticed him staring at her. Without a word, she slid onto his staff, encasing him inside her warm flesh. Her knees splayed on either side of his hips as she rocked back and forth.

"Woman, you are going to kill me."

Laughing, she squeezed his cock with her inner walls. "But what a pleasant way to go."

"Don't I know it." Antonius grabbed her waist and shoved her up and down on his cock, plunging his stiff flesh to the hilt into her wet heat.

Madria leaned over him, her hair a silken curtain that encased their faces. He took a breast in each hand and squeezed gently. In this position they seemed bigger, which excited him even more. Pulling her forward, he sucked a rosy nipple to an excited nub.

"Suck harder," she panted.

Antonius complied, applying more pressure with his mouth.

Madria groaned and pushed herself down hard on his cock. Arching backwards, she circled her hips, and the deep contact set his balls on fire. The sensation of her hot, soft flesh grinding against him was exquisite.

Her vagina tightened as her muscles spasmed. Antonius enjoyed watching her expressive face as she climaxed. Her pink tongue licked her lower lip, while her eyes remained closed.

He had wanted their lovemaking to last longer, but the look on Madria's face and the stroke of her inner walls set him off. Shards of pleasure lanced through his cock as he rammed upward, releasing his seed in several forceful bursts.

A sudden wind whipped through the trees, bringing with it sprinkling drops. They hadn't even noticed the impending storm. Grabbing their clothes, the throw, and the clay, they ran inside.

The air became chilly quickly and Antonius started a fire in the hearth. Sitting side by side, they stared into the flames. Listening, he got up and opened the door. Without much hope, he called for his cat.

"Perhaps she found a new home," Madria said softly.

Shrugging, he closed the door. "I hope so," he muttered under his breath. He hated to think of his sweet cat lying dead somewhere.

Madria turned to peer nervously at each clap of lightning. Returning to the hearth, he placed an arm about her shoulders and sought to soothe her with stories.

It worked somewhat, but Madria seemed fearful of the lightning and thunder. Maybe she was recalling the storm that brought her to him. Finally, he took her hand and crawled into bed. She snuggled against his chest, but her body twitched at each thunderclap.

He knew what he must do. Turning her face up, he placed a tender kiss to her lips. Madria returned his kiss eagerly. After he stroked her tongue and sucked on her lower lip, she relaxed into his arms.

Moving downward, he laved one nipple. She arched up, ignoring the boom of thunder outside.

Madria clung to his shoulders. She trembled as a loud clap of thunder erupted overhead. Sexual excitement had not distracted her yet.

Foregoing the extended caressing he usually liked to engage in, Antonius pulled her legs apart and entered her in one thrust. She released a breath and shifted her hips.

"Antonius, I need you," she moaned.

"And I, you." He kissed her, his cock growing even harder at the whimpering moans beneath his lips.

He draped her legs over his shoulders and slid back and forth slowly. Madria cried out as he penetrated her deeply, loving the tight feeling of her hot, wet flesh clamped around his cock. A few more strokes and he eased her legs back down and captured her mouth, demanding her surrender.

The thunder had receded some, so that Madria no longer started at each boom. But the air was charged with electricity. Tingles ran along his skin and he shivered as Madria's fingertips ran up and down his back.

Their kiss turned into one filled with hunger, their tongues dancing in slow, hot caresses. His blood boiled and an unexpected savage urge hit him. Antonius wanted all of her — her lips, breasts, pussy, and her love. It was as if the lightning zinged along his nerve endings, turning him into a ravenous beast.

The storm raged at a distance while he tried to control the fierce sensations inside him, and use them for their mutual pleasure.

Chapter Thirteen

"Madria," he groaned, ramming into her, desiring her shuddering response.

The lightning cracked, and by her arched body and cry of pleasure, she felt the same lancing shards of electricity that coursed through his blood. She twisted beneath him, grinding her pussy against his cock.

"Madria," he bellowed as his cock filled with his seed, and then gushed into her soft flesh with force.

"Oh," she whimpered. But then her channel convulsed and she pulled his hips back and forth, increasing the tempo.

Goose bumps ran along his arms as he slowed to a gentle thrusting.

Madria pulled his mouth down and gave him a tender, wet kiss. "That was wonderful."

"Yes, my love, it was special."

He kissed her deeply, one born of love, not lust. Stretching out beside her, he pulled her into his arms. They both fell asleep that way, completely sated and happy.

* * * * *

The next day, after finishing his gardening, Antonius worked on the figurine of Madria.

It took a week for him to complete the statue to his satisfaction. During break times, he and Madria made love wildly, as if each encounter were the first time.

Sitting and contemplating the figurine's sleek lines, Antonius was happy. Here were the slim lines and feline beauty he had sought to imbue into his other statue.

"What do you think?" he turned and asked as Madria walked up.

She squatted next to him and traced one finger along the curves. "Very lovely."

Antonius handed her his only other tunic, which she had stripped off for the posing. Madria grimaced and slipped it back on, scratching at the wool over her stomach.

"Would you like another linen tunic to wear?"

"Yes, oh yes." She smiled widely.

"Then it is about time I take a trip into town." He glanced toward the house. "That exquisite little statue might fetch enough for linen material."

After refilling the water gourd and packing a few food supplies into a bag, all that was left was carefully packing the figurine. Tying the food bag and gourd to his left side, he held the bag containing the statue securely with his right hand. It was the diminutive statue that had sat in the corner for months. The one he had never been satisfied with until he carved Madria's form. *That* creation he was very proud of and would never sell.

"Ready to go?"

Madria nodded. Her eyes sparkled with excitement, but she also had a nervous look on her face. Antonius wandered if the Po River valley could be her homeland. Many rich noblemen lived along its fringes, so the chances of him running into her previously would have been slim, especially since he rarely went there. The village nearby usually was quite adequate for his needs, but Po provided a better opportunity for sale of his artwork. It was famous for its lovely statues and frescoes.

Po was a full day's walk in distance, but Madria kept up with him easily. In fact, she seemed to enjoy the trek immensely. They stopped on the outskirts of town and camped for the night.

Sitting around the campfire was very pleasant and they cuddled atop the lambskin throw. The next morning, they arose at sunrise so Antonius could get set up early in the market.

Madria was fine until they entered the market square, which was already filled with shoppers. Then she clung to his arm and acted very skittish. Perhaps she didn't like crowds.

Antonius found a nice spot between two merchants. A space too small for the carts most pulled up to sell their wares from, but large enough for him to spread his throw. He set the small statue in the center of the rug then stood near the front. That way, he could catch previous customers' eyes, and keep any clumsy patrons from stepping on his figurine.

People wandered by, a few stopping out of curiosity. But most passed on to the carts containing fresh vegetables, fruit, cooking wares, and fabric. The sun was shining fiercely overhead, and Antonius was becoming disheartened. He shifted anxiously back and forth. It was nearly noon.

Madria had long ago sat cross-legged on the back end of the throw. Her eyes still flitted to the hurrying bodies passing by, but now more with interest than anxiety.

He was ready to eat lunch, when he recognized a portly body coming his way. Ah, Fautus. The rich landowner had purchased several statues through the years to grace his home.

"Antonius." Fautus clapped him on the shoulder. "Good lad, what lovely art have you brought today?"

He stepped aside and waved toward the figurine. Fautus' beady eyes barely flicked over the clay form before eying Madria far too closely.

"A slave? I'd be interested in bidding for such a beauty."

"No slave." Antonius' jaw clenched. Just the man asking, made his blood boil. "My cousin," he added to ward off any further questions.

Fautus shrugged and asked to see the statue. Turning it in his meaty hands, he exclaimed over its fine lines. Antonius knew he'd overreacted to the man's interest. Slave trading was common even in this small town.

At first, he had thought to gain several customers' attention in order to get a better price. But Fautus' enthusiasm for

Madria's beauty changed his mind. The thought of more old perverts ogling Madria like a succulent treat sickened him. He quickly settled on a reasonable amount and was glad when the large man left reluctantly.

Rolling the rug up, he slung it on his back, with a string holding it in place. Taking Madria's hand, he asked, "Want to do a little shopping?"

Nodding, she eagerly kept up with his stride. Barely glancing at the vegetable or fruit carts, she tugged his hand when they neared a man cooking pig meat over a fire. He was selling large hunks of the aromatic meat. Antonius bought one for each of them, and they nibbled the delicious flesh off the stick on which it had been cooked.

After they washed their hands in the central fountain, he strolled hand-in-hand with Madria to the cart selling fabric. Running their hands over the various materials was fun. Antonius let a swatch of silk fall from his fingers. How he wished he could afford such luxury for Madria.

The next merchant had several different linen pieces. He picked out a pure white that he could afford. Plunking the last of his coins into the merchant's palm, he turned to Madria and held out the fabric. "Do you like?"

She took the linen and rubbed her face into it. "I love it." She kissed him softly. "Thank you."

They spent the rest of the afternoon wandering the market and the tiny, winding streets of the town. Once they headed out, Madria seemed most happy.

"Did you enjoy today?"

"Yes." She plucked a pink flower from the roadside, twirling it between her fingers. "But I'm glad we're going home."

Home. A shaft of joy shot through his heart at her words. Madria considered his home hers too. Did that mean she had decided to stay? Although she had acted nervous about going to Po, no one had spoken to her or seemed to recognize her. Of course she had drawn much attention, which he only expected due to her extraordinary beauty.

They were on the less traveled road when a huge brute of a man staggered toward them. Clearly, he was drunk, and occasionally pulled a long drink from a goatskin flask.

"Hey, pretty lady, want a drink?" The man had stopped in the middle of the small road, blocking their way.

Antonius didn't like the way the man's eyes crawled all over Madria, even worse than Fautus had done.

Madria simply shook her head at the man's question and edged closer to Antonius.

"Come on. I can show you a good time tonight." The man thrust his arm out and pulled her into his embrace.

"Get your hands off her, you great oaf." Antonius had never been so angry in his life—except for what had happened to Madria in the woods.

The man laughed loudly and took another swig.

Madria, who had been ignored by them both for a few seconds, hissed. The man stared in surprise. The next instant, he staggered back when she raked her nails across his face.

Chapter Fourteen

Antonius leaped forward as the man yelped, but not in time to stop him from backhanding her. Madria fell in a heap and he knelt to make sure she was all right. He touched her cheek tenderly. "Are you all right?"

She nodded and he kissed her quickly. "Wait right here."

Antonius sprang up and punched the man on the jaw. Shaking his head, the brute grinned and swung hard. Antonius stepped swiftly to the side. The drunk's wild swing put him off balance and he wobbled. As his body turned in a circle, Antonius placed his foot on the man's rump and pushed forcefully.

The man fell like a dead tree and lay there. He nudged the man's side—no movement.

"Is he dead?" Madria had walked up beside him.

"Looks like he passed out."

"Too bad." She shrugged.

He laughed, sure she didn't mean it. "Better get going; it will be dark soon."

They picked out a campsite not too far from where they'd slept the night before. Madria snuggled into his arms as soon as they bedded down.

"You saved me." She caressed his chest.

"Not exactly," he chuckled and rubbed her arm.

"You fought him."

"Hmmm…a punch and shove down."

She kissed his chin. "Still, he was a giant and you attacked him."

"I would protect you from anything in the human realm." His thoughts flitted back to his failure in protecting Madria from that god. He had to admit, it made him feel somewhat better to succeed this time.

"You make me feel so loved." Madria played with the hair on his chest.

Antonius turned her face up. The fire was still blazing and he could see her features easily.

"You are loved." He kissed her lips gently. "From the moment you fell through my door, it is as if I've always known you. Falling in love seemed only natural."

Her eyes shimmered with held-in tears. He couldn't tell if she were sad or happy. "And how do you feel?"

"Antonius, I have always loved you."

Those tears slid slowly down her satiny cheeks.

"What's the matter?" He wiped them away tenderly. "Is loving me such a bad thing?" Smiling, he tried to soften the seriousness of the question.

Shaking her head, Madria took a deep, shaky breath. "What if something happened to come between us?"

"I won't let it. Whatever worries you, I can handle it."

Her gaze was doubtful, so he added, "I know one way so no one can come between us. Marry me."

"Marry you… Can I do that?" Her expression was confused.

Antonius smiled reassuringly. "All you have to do is say yes."

She stared into his eyes. "Then I say yes."

"Good. As soon as we get home, we'll start making arrangements." Kissing her more deeply, he whispered against her lips, "Then you'll be mine forever."

"Forever," she whispered back.

But the doubt he heard in her voice made him wonder anew just what she was so fearful of.

* * * * *

Once they reached home, Madria seemed more at ease in the familiar setting. She joined him in planning their wedding with enthusiasm. It was going to be simple—a small gathering of close friends, food and wine.

His dear friend Decimus was very generous. Upon getting the personal invitation, he offered to supply all the wine. The small vineyard his friend owned helped supplement his farming income. Antonius grew grapes too, but not enough to make the quantity of wine that would be needed for festivities.

Taking most of the money he had stashed for less hardy times, he purchased a pig from a neighbor. Claudius gave him an extremely good deal—his wedding present to them. Antonius saved enough to put back some of the coins. Other invited guests insisted on bringing bread and cheese.

So, come the day of the event, there was plenty of food and wine for everyone. And it had not taken the last of his resources to make it a memorable day.

It was a breathtakingly beautiful day. There were a few fluffy clouds floating across the azure sky, and a light breeze made the air refreshing. Even the temperature was pleasant.

Right after they had returned from Po, Antonius had started working on Madria's new tunic. It had not surprised him that she didn't know how to sew. It did surprise him that she had a sudden change in heart about helping him around the farm. She followed him out to the garden and actually became good at weeding. She hauled water to help saturate his plants, gathered wild berries, and picked fruit off his trees. And in contrast, her naps became an infrequent occurrence. He wondered if knowing she was to be his wife had put this zest into her heart.

Today was their wedding day, and Madria wore the white tunic. With her long black hair waving in a flowing mass down her back, and a wreath of white flowers on her crown, she looked ethereal. She was a little nervous meeting his neighbors, but he held her hand and did the introductions.

Not one of his friends had met her yet, and were clearly shocked by her beauty. They also wondered where she came from. To fend them off, Antonius named a far-off village. The next question was how did they meet? That was easily answered by stating Madria was visiting relatives in Vene.

Although his friends might wonder at the suddenness of their marriage, they didn't question the love between them. Anyone glancing at them could see the happiness radiating from them both. And no one knew Madria had been living with him either.

The priest had arrived early since he walked from Vene. Although only a village, Vene had a modest-sized temple in honor of Venus, and Silvio served there. He had been a solace to Antonius when his parents died. Years later, Antonius created a lovely statue of Venus for the temple. Their relationship was close and Silvio was only too happy to perform the ceremony.

Chapter Fifteen

Madria couldn't believe she was marrying Antonius today. Her life seemed constantly filled with new emotions and discoveries in the human realm. She kept expecting it to end at any moment—that one of the gods would show up and change her back. But they didn't.

When her master had declared his love, her heart felt like it would break out of her chest. She thought that surely at that point the gods would intervene. When she did not change to a cat, she began to wonder if the gods had forgotten about her.

Now, all of Antonius' friends had gathered to watch them wed. Madria was already nervous before the first person showed up and by the time all were present, she was ready to jump out of her skin. Even as a cat she had not liked strangers. Today she had to deal with a yard full of humans.

An old lady came up and patted her arm, making a remark about wedding jitters. She was probably right, but it didn't help her calm down a bit. The only thing that kept her from bolting for the woods was Antonius holding her hand almost the whole time.

Everything seemed to pass in a haze. The human wedding ceremony was a confusing affair. The man, Silvio, stood in front of her and Antonius, repeating long words of a ritualistic tone. After he finished, Silvio bound their wrists with a ribbon.

The neighbors cheered loudly and Antonius held her hand, facing them. Then he led her between two columns the people had formed. Pieces of bread pelted their bodies as they ran through the laughing crowd.

Thankfully, after that they were seated with informality at a table, the guests sitting at other tables scattered around them.

Flitting images of a wonderful feast flashed by, although Madria barely picked at the succulent swine meat. She felt like she did when she sensed an impending storm. Something was coming — and it wasn't pleasant.

A thunderous boom made her cringe and snap out of her fugue state. The humans were staring up at the sky, confused looks on their faces. The sky was clear. Madria trembled, remembering how the god in the forest had appeared in just such a manner.

Several bolts of lightning flashed overhead. The wedding guests chatted excitedly and a few jumped up. An electric charged energy flowed through her body and abruptly two figures appeared in the center of the yard.

Madria shivered violently and clutched Antonius' hands. Those were the same two gods who had been arguing when she was changed to a human. A black shroud of sorrow hit her stomach. The gods had not forgotten her after all.

Whispers flew like chaff in the wind, as the humans realized unearthly beings graced the wedding.

Antonius stood up slowly, took a few steps, and then plunged to his knees. "How may we serve you?"

They both ignored her master and the other humans, and began exchanging words. Phrases that sounded too familiar. It was the same senseless argument from when Madria first heard them. While they argued, the humans whispered about the way the two beings looked.

The god was so handsome no marble statue could come close to his male beauty. While the goddess was so lovely, not even a talented poet could hope to describe the fineness of her form. Golden light illuminated their lustrous skin, as if a small sun radiated from each.

Quivers ran along Madria's flesh and it was as if she were back under that dripping bush again. Her limbs refused to move this time too.

Suddenly, the goddess pointed an elegant finger near the table where she sat, and a zap of lightning popped from her fingertips. A cloud of dust erupted and when it cleared, a tiny field mouse appeared.

Now that was something Madria could direct her attention to and distract her from the arguing beings. Everything around her didn't matter the frightened humans or the two disagreeable immortals. The mouse was reality—something familiar—something that brought a sense of security amongst all this chaos.

Getting up slowly, Madria ignored Antonius' startled look as she walked toward the mouse. She pounced, grasping the wiggling body in her hands.

Antonius was in total shock when the two figures suddenly appeared. At his wedding! Although he had never seen a god, he knew these two were. Stumbling up from the table, he plunged to his knees.

The god and goddess ignored his fearful plea and cast fierce words back and forth. It took several seconds for their conversation to sink in. His heart seemed to fall all the way to his stomach and he swallowed back sour bile. It wouldn't do to throw up in front of immortals.

Turning stunned eyes, he gazed at his lovely Madria. It *was* his Madria; had been all along. What a horrible trick the gods had played on him and his cat.

His sickness turned to horror as the mouse magically appeared and Madria jumped up. Antonius didn't know why, but inside his mind he screamed "no", while his lips were unable to utter a word.

Madria quickly caught the mouse. Immediately, the goddess let loose with a tinkling peal of laughter and pointed at his bride. Madria's form was sheathed in a hazy smoke and when it dissipated, his cat stood there, the mouse clutched in her mouth.

"No!" Antonius screamed, jumping to his feet.

The two gods disappeared in a dazzling display, their angry words hanging in the air for several seconds after they vanished. Madria ran off and hid under a bush, while his guests sat in silent shock.

After a minute, his friends began recovering from the experience. They surrounded him to give what comfort they could. A few thought the gods were jealous of Madria's beauty and in spite had turned her into a cat.

Antonius nodded numbly. It was a much better explanation than he could have come up with on his own. All the guests made excuses to slip quietly away, except for Decimus. His friend's wife kissed him and said she had to go home and start supper, but he knew she was leaving them alone.

At first he sat in silence, but after his friend handed him a fresh cup of wine, the dam burst. Antonius spilled the whole story in a rushing torrent of words. It felt comforting to have Decimus to talk with. Telling his friend also helped him absorb the truth about his two Madrias. All along he had known the human Madria was different but tried to make excuses for her strange behavior. It had often given him chills when he saw the similarities between the two. But his logical mind refused to believe the clues that had given him evidence of Madria's true self.

Antonius smiled to himself. Who would have believed such a thing? Although the gods were prayed to and talked about frequently, he had never seen one until his wedding day. He was sure none of his guests had either.

When Antonius finished his story, he could tell Decimus was surprised by his expression. But his consolatory words felt nice, even though they didn't help.

"What are you going to do?"

Antonius shook his head. "I don't know." He took a large gulp of wine. "Those two were playing with our lives—all because of a bet."

Decimus sighed. "Perhaps…if you prayed to them?"

"Yes," he sat up from his slumped position. "I must pray for her to change Madria back."

"Her?"

"The goddess is the one who bet Madria's cat nature would win out."

"Oh. I blanked out most of their conversation." Decimus looked puzzled.

"As did my other friends, it seems." He took another drink. "It's just as well, I'd rather no one but you know the true story."

"It shall never pass to another human being." He refilled his cup and then Antonius'. "But which goddess do you pray to?"

"I think…it was Venus." He stared at the spot where the gods had appeared. "She was too beautiful."

"I agree." Decimus stood. "Will you be all right?"

"Yes." Antonius got up and clapped his friend on the shoulder. "Thanks for staying, but it's time for you to go home to your pretty wife." He stared over Decimus' shoulder, into the woods. "And it's time for me to find Madria."

Chapter Sixteen

With a sad look in his eyes, his friend left. Antonius called to Madria over and over. He was about to give up for the night, when he noticed a small form huddled beneath a bush. Bending down, he spoke softly to her.

After a few seconds, his cat came to him slowly. Picking her up, he entered his house. Antonius sat in a chair and soothed her with strokes down her soft fur. Finally he scratched under Madria's chin and guided it upward so he could see her sweet kitty face. Her brilliant green eyes were confused and scared. At least, that was the expression he thought he saw.

Letting her head ease back down, Antonius continued to caress her fur while he struggled to contain his sorrow. He could feel tears gathering, but gritted his teeth. Taking a few deep breaths, he controlled his emotions. He wasn't ready for defeat yet, and was determined to get his lovely human Madria back.

Running his hand down his cat's back, he enjoyed listening to her purrs. Sadness lanced through him when he realized that if he regained his wife, he would lose his precious kitty. His hand paused. But not really, his mind whispered back. His human Madria had many of the cat's personality quirks.

Antonius was exhausted, his emotions wrung out. It was his wedding night, and he was brideless. Crawling into bed, he tried to sleep, but spent hours staring into the dark. Madria had chosen to ramble the house, reacquainting herself with it as a cat. When she seemed satisfied, she curled up against his chest. Finding her presence soothing, he finally drifted off to sleep.

The next morning, before he went out to his garden, Antonius prayed. On his knees for at least fifteen minutes, he implored the goddess for mercy. He had no way to tell if his prayers got through, but he felt more at peace while working. Antonius knew if his entreaties were heeded, it would take more than one time to gain Venus' attention.

As the days flowed into one another, he began to get frustrated and disheartened. Venus either wasn't listening or didn't care about his sorrow. Still hoping to catch her attention, he traveled twice a week to Vene to pray at her temple.

The statue he knelt before stood as cold as he felt his reception was from the goddess. Staring at the sculpture, Antonius got an idea. If Venus wouldn't listen to his prayers, would a gift appeal to her? The more he thought about it, the more he was convinced that making a statue in Venus' honor might gain her attention. Gods were known to be vain beings. And although the statue was nice and the very one he had created as a youth, he could do far more justice to a creation now.

Once arriving home, Antonius was happier than he'd been since the ill-fated wedding. He put a large piece of marble into the center of the room. It was a very lovely piece of stone, pure white with gold veins. He never could have afforded such expensive marble, but his richest patron in the area had given it to him.

Years ago, Liviana and her family had decided to visit relatives in Greece. Several of their servants had died of plague. Liviana had offered Antonius the position of servant. She knew he longed to gaze upon the exquisite Grecian statues. His parents had still been alive and had urged him to go. It would be a hardship on his elderly parents to take care of the farm by themselves, but they knew such an opportunity wouldn't come again.

Before returning home, Liviana had purchased three wonderful hunks of marble to take back with her. And she had hired a master sculptor to teach Antonius the art. Her plan was for him to sculpt a statue of her and Valerius, her husband.

Antonius had been overwhelmed by her generous gift, for that is what it was. She could have hired an artist already adept at carving marble into figures, but she had wanted him to do it. Liviana had always believed in his talent, and this had been her way of encouraging him to expand his artistic ability.

His training had taken a long time, and Liviana had extended her visit into almost a year to allow him that time. When they finally returned home, he had worked on the statues for his patron, in between his farming duties. It had been a hard task, but well worth the effort. Two beautiful statues now graced Liviana and Valerius' foyer—one of the handsome-featured woman and the other her portly husband.

The couple had been very pleased with the statues. One day, soon after he finished the creations, a wagon stopped at his farm. On its bed rested the third piece of marble. Liviana's servant said his mistress had instructed that Antonius do with it as he wished.

Liviana's servants had brought a sturdy wood-bottom platform with wheels underneath, on which the marble rested. He had thanked her later for her thoughtfulness in sending the platform. Although useful for moving the heavy piece of stone, he had not needed it. The marble had sat in the corner all this time.

It was a gift beyond measure, and until now, he had hesitated to make anything from it. Now he knew what to do with the marble. He would carve a statue to a patron beyond any he could have foreseen—Venus herself. That first day, he simply sat and stared at the lustrous stone, letting it speak to him.

The next day, he started carving the marble, allowing Venus' form to take shape gradually. He worked in the evening and Madria sat and watched attentively. Antonius found himself speaking to her as if she were still human. Madria would listen and occasionally answer with a meow. Her presence was comforting.

That night, he went to bed with less sorrow in his heart and a bit of hope. But his aloneness hit him even more. When would he get back his beloved bride?

Madria yowled to go outside and he had reluctantly let her out. He couldn't keep her a prisoner. As he lay there trying to relax, his mind latched onto heated exchanges they had shared and the feminine beauty of her body.

His cock hardened and he ran one hand over it lightly. Placing one hand around the shaft, he stroked up and down. Antonius moaned, then paused. This self-pleasure felt wrong when his bride was lost to him. The blood pounded in his flesh, ignoring his thoughts.

Thrusting aside his qualms, Antonius concentrated on human Madria's face. She smiled knowingly and reached out a hand. It was her palm that pumped his cock up and down.

After a few caresses, her head bent and he groaned as her tongue laved his flesh. It stroked from the tip, down the shaft, then back to the head. His fingers teased his cock's head as he imagined Madria sucking him.

Her mouth was hot, wet, and greedy. His hips rose up as he shoved his cock into her slurping mouth. He wanted her so badly. His hand moved fast and the blood pounded through his hardened flesh.

With a gurgling cry, he gushed his seed into her mouth. A sigh escaped him as the last of his liquid leaked out.

Staring into the dark room, Antonius was physically sated, but felt more alone than ever. Getting up, he cleaned up, then called for Madria. Thankfully, she came running. Cuddling with her warm body helped him become relaxed enough to sleep.

The next morning he whistled while doing his gardening. He was anxious to get started again on the statue, but restrained himself until his duties were done. Madria sat by his side that evening, watching him carve.

* * * * *

As the days turned into weeks, Antonius managed to keep his sadness at bay by concentrating on his creation. Madria seemed determined to stay with him, leaving only for short periods to hunt in the woods. Sometimes he glanced at her green eyes and thought he saw a flicker of understanding. He wondered how much of her previous life she remembered, if any at all.

Finally, after months of careful sculpting, the statue stood in the middle of the room—finished. Antonius examined it with a critical artist's eyes. It was the exquisite piece he had envisioned. He took a deep breath. Would Venus think it a masterpiece as well?

The following morning he walked to Vene and spoke with the priest. Silvio was very excited that he had carved a new statue for the temple and arranged to send a wagon the next day.

When the wagon arrived, Antonius was pleased to see the priest as well as two servants. The marble was very heavy and two men couldn't have lifted it onto the wagon. Liviana's platform came in very handy, making the transport from the house to the wagon feasible.

"Antonius, you have outdone yourself." Silvio was ecstatic. "The goddess will be pleased."

He certainly hoped Venus would be happy, otherwise all that hard work had been for nothing.

Carefully moving the statue out to the wagon wasn't too difficult because of the platform. But it took all four of them to lift the statue onto the wagon. Silvio had brought blankets, which were piled on the wagon bed, making it cushiony. The priest tied ropes across the marble in several places, securing it firmly.

Antonius waved goodbye to the priest, hope in his heart. Each evening he prayed to the goddess. Weeks went by and nothing changed.

He was totally disheartened. It was a month later and that morning he picked at his food, having little appetite. Opening the door to go to his garden, he was surprised to see the priest walking briskly toward him.

"Antonius." The priest clapped him on the shoulders. "You must come back to the temple."

"Why?" He could barely summon enough interest to ask that question.

"Your statue has created a sensation."

Chapter Seventeen

"What do you mean?" Antonius' lost interest sprang to life.

"Word has spread about your wonderful statue. People are making pilgrimages to pray to Venus."

"That's nice. I hope they are getting their prayers answered." He couldn't keep the sarcasm from his voice.

"My boy, don't give up hope." Silvio put an arm around his shoulders. "Please come to the temple two days hence. We're having a special celebration to welcome the new statue. The creator should be there."

He shrugged. "I'll see."

The priest left shortly after, and Antonius had to admit the invitation was appealing. He put it from his mind, or tried to. No matter what chore he set himself, his thoughts revolved back to the ethereal statue he had made.

Two days later, he quit trying to convince himself he wasn't interested in the celebration. Inside, he was dying of curiosity to see the sensation the statue had created.

The walk to Vene was pleasant, and it felt good to stretch his legs. Antonius was shocked when he neared the temple and saw the huge crowd of people. Everyone was clothed in their best finery, the women wearing flower wreaths in their hair. Long tables laden with food had been set between the tall columns.

Villagers he knew spotted him as he approached the entrance and patted his back. Cries of "Antonius—the creator" rose from many throats. He had to push through the throng. The crowd parted once he went through the atrium and he walked past the cheering, smiling faces. There she stood. Venus.

The statue was on a raised dais in the center of the temple. The dais was a recent addition since it had not been there the last time he visited. Tall candles set in even taller candle holders, ringed the statue, casting a golden glow on her figure. It almost made her look real. Antonius took in a sharp breath. He'd forgotten how lovely she was.

Not sure what to do, he was glad to see the priest coming toward him. Silvio welcomed him and stood next to Antonius as he intoned a long prayer. The temple was hushed as the crowd stilled their movements and chatter.

When his prayer was finished, Silvio spoke to those who had traveled far. People pushed in close, some just to touch Antonius' tunic. The congratulations were nice, but the fawning behavior made him ill at ease. Saying a quick goodbye to the priest, he slipped out.

On the walk home, hope grew anew in his heart. Perhaps Venus would hear the prayers of so many. Maybe she would come to see her statue and turn her favor upon him.

Antonius kicked a stone in his path. He didn't really believe that. The faint ray of hope dissolved as quickly as it had erupted.

Venus was gazing in a gilded hand mirror, trying to decide if she liked the new hairdo her servant had arranged. A nymph skipped gaily into her presence. She would have been annoyed by the intrusion into her bower, but Daphne was her favorite.

"What brings you here?" Venus tried to keep a stern expression, a hard thing to do when faced by such a cheerful creature.

"I thought you should know, great Venus, that your deity is being worshiped most fervently."

"What nonsense. I am always worshiped." Venus waved a hand of dismissal.

The nymph giggled and spun in a circle. "Yes, but in the village of Vene, many humans are making pilgrimages to your temple there."

"They are?" She became more interested. "And how would you know this?"

"Because many pilgrims pass through my woods going and returning, and I hear them talk."

Venus knew there was more and her curiosity was raging, but she would not lower herself to ask.

"A new statue has been placed in the temple at Vene," the sprite whispered, as if it were a big secret.

"So," she scoffed. "I have countless statues erected to my beauty."

"But none like this one." Daphne's eyes shone with excitement. "The talk is of a statue so wondrous, no other can touch its loveliness."

"I must see this statue." Venus threw down her mirror and ran one hand down Daphne's hair. She clicked her fingers and conjured an orange from her garden, giving it to the nymph. Of course it was no ordinary fruit and the nymph laughed with happiness.

Venus materialized in the temple. It was night, so she need not worry about being spotted by a mortal. The marble figure was center stage, surrounded by candles, still alight, washing the statue in a soft glow. Stretching out a finger, she touched the cool stone.

Shaking her head, Venus was surprised and pleased. It looked just like her, down to her sultry curves and the angular lines of her face. With the light playing over the form, it almost could be real.

A soft footstep made her turn sharply. A priest. She had thought to dematerialize before being seen, but one of her temple servants was a welcome sight.

"Priest." Venus used her Olympian voice.

The man saw her and fell to his knees, looking ready to faint.

Pointing to the statue, she asked, "Who made this?"

The priest trembled and gave her a name, even telling her where the artist lived.

Venus reappeared, but as an invisible vapor, in the small house belonging to Antonius. He was a handsome young man. He was sitting by the hearth, staring at a small statue. It too was exquisite, but of course did not compare to her own effigy. Beside the artist sat a black cat, staring at the statue too.

Antonius looked so morose it touched her heart. Coming closer, she leaned down and saw a tear slide down his cheek. What could cause such sorrow in a young man?

Glancing back at the statue, she realized there was something familiar about it. Venus' eyes went back and forth, between the young man and the statue, then even to the cat. A scene flashed through her mind — a wedding and a bet with Jupiter.

A funny feeling ran through her and it took a few seconds to realize that it was guilt. Venus rarely experienced this emotion. She did not like it.

The feline turned its green eyes in her direction. Venus stared eye to eye with the beast. Animals had such attuned senses, sometimes they could see a god, even if the immortal were invisible. Those brilliant green orbs seemed to accuse.

Venus was about to return to Olympus when she remembered the unearthly beauty of Antonius' creation. Her heart softened.

How angry she had been at Jupiter when she found out he had played seducer to the cat-maiden. Few secrets could be kept from the wood nymphs. She had only felt it justified to make a mouse appear at the wedding.

Yet this young man sat, steeped in sorrow because the gods had played with his life. What did he do? Made a statue so lovely the other gods would envy her. Venus smiled. That thought made her happy. Jupiter would never have a statue to rival hers.

Waving an arm toward her body, she took a deep whiff of the air surrounding the man. She could read from his body that he had been sending fervent prayers for her help. She had not listened, but she did now. Every pore in her body responded to his lost love.

With a wave of her hand she materialized in front of the man. His eyes widened, but otherwise he sat frozen in place. The cat hissed, but did not run.

"Antonius, I have seen the statue you made in my honor, and I am pleased." Pointing to the cat, she changed the beast back into a human.

Fading to her invisible state, she watched in real pleasure as the two embraced. Such joy was usually seen only in Olympus.

Venus smiled and returned in a flash to her home. The news of her generosity would spread among the gods and Jupiter would have another reason to be jealous of her. Venus' tinkling laughter followed her all the way home.

Chapter Eighteen

Antonius was so shocked when Venus appeared, he couldn't budge a muscle. Only after she magically dissolved, could he move. Jumping up, he grabbed Madria in a big hug and danced around the room with her in his arms. He was crying and laughing with joy at the same time, and so was his bride.

Finally, he paused and simply looked into her lovely eyes.

"Oh, Antonius, I missed talking with you." She caressed his face with both hands.

"Me too…and other things."

"Yes," she sighed. "Kiss me." Madria opened her mouth and licked her bottom lip.

He captured her lush lips in a sweet kiss to begin with, then ran his tongue along her lower lip. She moaned as his tongue slipped inside her mouth, stroking her tongue.

Antonius ached for her body so badly it was as if he'd never made love to her before. Their kiss turned into something wild, driven by their mutual need for each other. Her hands tore at his tunic and he helped, ripping it at one shoulder.

Madria was nude and he pulled her slim curves to his body in a tight hold, wanting to feel every inch of her velvety skin.

"Yes, oh, yes." She kneaded his shoulders, and then her nails raked down his skin. "Touch me all over." Her head fell back weakly as he caressed her breasts.

His hands stroked down to her hips, and then gripping them, he rammed his inflamed cock into her belly. Her head came up and she panted, wiggling her lower body against him.

"I have missed touching you," he said as his hands slid around to her cute ass and kneaded it. Turning her, he pulled Madria's backside against his groin.

She rubbed her butt back and forth, until his cock pounded.

"What else have you missed?" her words hissed out between breaths.

"Kissing you." He threw her hair to the side and kissed her neck.

She groaned and her movements stilled.

"Tasting you." Antonius licked her neck in one long stroke.

She panted and threw her head back onto his shoulder.

"Making love to you," he whispered in her ear before catching the lobe in his mouth.

Madria groaned. He moved one hand to her breast, exciting the already hardened nipple more with his fingers, while his other hand slipped down her body. His fingers splayed over her mons and he slowly slid a forefinger between her lower lips. Madria's hips shoved upward, encasing his finger fully in her folds. She was hot and slick with her own juices.

Her soft whimpers surged through his blood, setting him on fire. Skimming his finger up and down the folds, he was gratified by her pumping hips that moved in rhythm to his caresses. Each time she moved, his cock was pressed into the crevice of her buttocks. Antonius moaned and slipped his finger into her channel. It clamped around his finger as he gently stroked.

Madria's panting breath pulled him closer to the boiling point. Withdrawing his finger, he slicked through her warm moistness and then found the clit.

"Ah," she moaned, her hips stilling. "Make me come for you," she gasped as shudders gripped her.

Knowing what would throw her over the edge, he nuzzled the side of her neck, licking and nipping, inhaling her unique scent before he bit and held her. Picking up the speed of his caresses on her sensitive nub, he was satisfied by her excited moans. Sucking the flesh into his mouth, while he flicked her clit rapidly, pushed her into an orgasm.

Madria screamed and he almost lost his grip on her throat, but continued to lave her skin as his finger stroked her nub, riding out the orgasm.

"Stop," she moaned, her head flopping weakly onto his shoulder.

Antonius wrapped his arms around her waist and then repositioned their bodies next to the bed. Without saying a word, he bent her over, his hands running over her velvety skin. He nibbled a path down her delicate spine, licking the small of her back. Madria sighed heavily and her hands dug into the mattress. She flung her hair back and forth, caressing his face with the silken tresses.

"You are so soft, so beautiful." His voice came out husky as he barely contained control of his raging cock. It throbbed, ached to be inside her.

Madria spread her legs, her cute ass rising up to meet the nudging of his staff at her entrance. Moving with supple grace, she reached between her legs and guided him to her wet flesh.

His cock edged into her entrance and he paused for a few seconds, soaking up the sensation of her hot wetness against the head. Then holding his staff, he eased slowly inside her.

"I must have you, my sweet." Antonius slid all the way, his balls slapping against her mons. "I thought never to touch you again—as a human."

Madria thrust her ass backwards, ramming her pussy onto his engorged flesh. "Feel me, my love. I am real—as human as any woman."

"Yes," he groaned, gripping her hips and pulling them back and forth. Their skin made wet sucking sounds, exciting him further. Leaning over, he slipped one hand under her and stroked her sensitive clit as his cock moved gently inside her.

"Yes, that's it," she moaned, circling her pussy.

Pulling back, he plunged in slowly, making Madria quiver.

She laid her head flat on the bed, causing her cute butt to raise even more. Antonius shoved in, increasing his tempo.

"Harder," she screamed.

His strokes became one long thrust after another. He ground his cock into her flesh, eliciting little whimpering moans from her. Running his hands around her breasts, he brought her body up. His front completely covered her backside. The contact of her velvety flesh sliding against him, made his breathing increase and his cock grow harder. Catching on to the new position with enthusiasm, Madria bounced up and down on his cock. His hands on her waist moved her body with more force.

She was so tight and hot he felt ready to come, but held back with an effort. He wanted Madria to come around him, reach her pleasure first. Slipping one hand to her right breast, he squeezed it and then rolled the hard nipple, while his other hand moved down. Intent on filling her completely, he worked two fingers into her folds, her fluid easing his entry as they glided in alongside his stroking cock.

"Oh," she groaned.

Her inner muscles clenched as an orgasm flushed through her pussy. Antonius continued slow, long strokes of his cock as he ran his fingers through her moist flesh. The spasm of her pussy pulled at him and his sperm erupted, shooting into her greedy channel with force.

They fell, exhausted, onto the mattress. Once she snuggled into his arms, Antonius relaxed completely. He didn't fall asleep, but could have chuckled when he heard her soft breathing. Madria had not lost her ability to fall asleep easily.

He hoped she would retain some of her quirky cat characteristics. He loved her purring, and the way she cuddled up against him like a kitten. But most of all, he was thrilled with her sexual responsiveness. Madria was always ready for sex, as if she were constantly in heat. He smiled. Perhaps that was a strange carryover from her feline origins.

"A kiss for your thoughts?" She spoke softly from beneath his arm. Her head rested on his chest while his arms were wrapped around her shoulders.

"How about just a kiss?" Leaning down he gave her a long, wet kiss.

She broke contact and her lower lip stuck out. "You always told me your thoughts when I was a cat."

Antonius laughed. "Okay... I didn't mean to keep anything from you, my inquisitive girl." He shrugged. "I was simply thinking of how I loved some of your cat qualities."

"Like?"

"Your purring."

She distracted him by purposely purring loudly. "Um, then your enjoyment of sex."

Madria giggled and slid down his body. Not sure exactly what she was up to, his breath hitched when her hair smoothed over his cock. He watched as she nudged his half-hard staff with her nose, then placing her lips against it, she purred again loudly.

Tiny vibrations ran from her lips into his quickly hardening flesh. It felt strange, almost ticklish, but also very good. Her long, pink tongue flicked out and swiped at the head.

"Madria, it's dirty." One hand tangled in her hair, but he didn't push her away.

"Mmm, I know." With that statement, she opened her mouth wide and took his whole length in one downward swoop.

Chapter Nineteen

Antonius gasped. It was so damn hot and wet, reminding him of her sweet pussy. He shoved upward, mimicking a fucking motion. Madria bobbed up and down in time with his rhythm.

Suddenly, she halted all movement, but kept him in her mouth. Watching her, he was surprised when a thrumming sensation hit his cock, encasing it in vibrations.

"Oh, gods, Madria," he groaned. She was purring very deeply, stirring his flesh into new levels of excitement.

Withdrawing her mouth a bit, she kept only the head inside. Again, she purred, hitting his aching cock with tiny pulsations.

His breathing increased and his stomach tightened. Continuing her purring, Madria added to the erotic massage, stroking her tongue around the tip.

"Argh," Antonius yelled, his hand gripping a handful of her hair. His balls felt like rocks and his seed poured into her waiting mouth in a hot stream.

After a few more pumps of his fluid, he looked at her. She plopped him from her mouth, her eyes never leaving his face as she licked every droplet from the head.

It took a full minute before his sated flesh calmed. Kissing his flaccid cock, she edged up his body and took up her favorite cuddling position.

"You are going to kill me, woman."

She laughed and tickled the hair on his chest. "Rest, we have much more sexual heat before us."

He took a deep breath. She was right. Unbelievably, he was still as hungry for her as the first time they made love. His eyes closed and he became drowsy.

Antonius awoke later, glad she was still asleep. He wanted to surprise her with a special wake-up kiss. Carefully, he knelt beside her legs. Madria was curled on her side and he slowly eased her onto her back. Holding his position, he was glad when she didn't awaken.

Contemplating her thighs, he wondered if pushing them apart would wake her. Satisfaction ran through him when she mumbled and splayed her legs. Perfect.

Repositioning between her spread thighs, he gazed at the dark pink lips nestled between the black pubic hairs. Plump and delicious looking.

Gently, he pulled her lips apart. Madria mumbled but slept on. His nose pushed between her soft folds and his tongue found her clit. Her fragrance made his cock jump to life and the moist flavor of her feminine juices made him ache. How he wanted her, and knew he'd never tire of her essence.

The tiny nub hardened beneath his strokes, pushing upward to meet his tongue. Madria muttered and moved restlessly. Antonius smiled into her slick folds. She would have a very pleasant awakening.

His tongue circled her clit, but then he decided it was time for Madria to be aware of what was happening to her. Stiffening his tongue, he flicked at the nub with fast strokes.

"Antonius," she moaned, and her hands ran through his hair. "Oh, oh," she screamed. Her hips shoved upward and her hands pushed his head deeper into her flesh.

Antonius continued his licks, enjoying the excited whimpers from his wife. He could actually feel her nub throbbing beneath his caresses. Only when she began pushing him away, did he stop.

"My love," she wiggled her fingers, urging him into her arms. "That was heavenly." She pushed her head up to capture his lips. She literally ravished his mouth, her licks and nibbles demanding his surrender.

It was an odd thought, surrendering to a woman, but he liked it.

Shoving at his chest and detaching her lips, she said, "Lie down. Let me pleasure you, my husband."

He stretched out on his back and Madria positioned herself over his half-hard cock. Her lower lips slipped around his aroused flesh as she glided back and forth. In a few strokes it was ready for her. Smiling, she wiggled until his cock plunged inside her pussy.

Madria placed her hands on his chest, tweaking his nipples while her hips rocked. The blood in his veins felt like fire raced along them.

"Come here." He pulled her to his lips. They kissed deeply, their love shining through the heat igniting between them.

Rearing back, she whispered, "Suck them," then pulled his face toward her and pushed one breast into his mouth.

Antonius placed one hand on each breast, and then sucked on a nipple. He loved the texture of her pebbled skin and the way she moaned as he suckled. His cock pounded, sheathed to the hilt in her wet silky flesh.

"Yes," she gasped, shoving her hardened nub deeper into his mouth.

Swiveling her hips, Madria rotated her pussy faster and faster. A string of sizzling electric-charged sensation was attached from his mouth to his balls that made his balls clench.

Their lovemaking increased in tempo, razing his body with excitement so strong, his legs trembled. She was a wild creature, riding him with savage enthusiasm, while he thrust into her flesh just as fiercely.

Gazing into her lovely eyes, his orgasm ravaged him, and he bellowed her name aloud. All the muscles in his body seemed to go rigid in reaction, while Madria bucked atop him, like a rider on a stallion.

She stopped all movement abruptly and, arching her back, made a strangling sound. Her pussy continued to move gently, milking the last of his seed. Her head flopped back toward him and she stared at him.

"Will it always be so wonderful — this sexual heat between us?"

"Yes." He pulled her down into his arms and she snuggled on his chest. That was a big statement to live up to, but he didn't want anything negative coming between them right now.

Antonius was so happy it seemed unreal. His thoughts went back over the previous weeks. "I thought I'd never get you back. I prayed to Venus faithfully, but she didn't listen."

"I know." She stretched upward and placed a kiss to his chin. "It was the statue that changed her mind."

Cocking his head, he stared at her. "How much were you aware of as a cat?"

She shrugged. "Bits and pieces. But I knew you were sad about losing human Madria. I watched you carve the statue." She stared at the wall. "I didn't know why you made it or the importance, until Venus appeared today."

He hugged her close. "Will you miss being a cat?"

Madria smiled. "Some. I'll miss being able to slink quietly through the underbrush, chasing mice, and other things." She ran her nails playfully over his arm. "There are other, very pleasant things I would have missed more if I had stayed a cat."

"Really? Like what?" He stroked one of her breasts, pleased by her indrawn breath.

Her face scrunched up. "Oh, like taking naps."

He circled her nipple. "I don't think that's what you meant, you minx."

She giggled. "Actually, I was getting tired of napping so much."

"You are good at changing the subject," he sighed in an exaggerated fashion. "I thought you enjoyed naps?"

"Strangely, the longer I stayed human, the more boring it became." She propped up on one elbow, her black hair cascading around her. "I even started liking gardening."

Antonius raised one eyebrow. "Hmmm, I didn't notice the *liking*, but you did start helping me."

She pushed against his chest and snorted. "Anyway, I lived part of my life as a cat and enjoyed it very much. Now it is time for me to explore life fully as a human."

Madria stared at him, catching his eyes. "Antonius, do you know I haven't seen a temple? I'd love to see your statue inside Venus' temple."

He nodded. "Sure, we can go tomorrow if you wish."

She snuggled into his arms. "So many things to discover, I barely know where to begin."

Leaning over her, he whispered huskily, "You can start by exploring all the many ways to make love."

She giggled. "I thought we had."

"Not all." He closed her lips with a kiss.

About the author:

Myra Nour grew up reading s/f, fantasy, and romance, so she was really thrilled when these elements were combined in Futuristic Romances. She enjoys writing within all these elements, whether the hero is a handsome man from another planet, or a tiny fairy from another dimension.

Myra's background is in counseling, and she likes using her knowledge to create believable characters. She also enjoys lively dialogue and, of course, using her imagination to create other worlds with lots of action/adventure, as well as romance. She uses her handsome husband as inspiration for her heroes - he is a body builder, a soldier, and has a black belt in Tae Kwon Do.

Myra welcomes mail from readers. You can write to her c/o Ellora's Cave Publishing at 1056 Home Avenue, Akron Ohio 44310-3502.

Also by Myra Nour:

As You Wish
Future Lost 1: A Mermaid's Longing
Mystic Visions
Shifter's Desire 1: Vampire Fangs and Venom

Pussyfooting Around

Ashley Ladd

Trademarks Acknowledgement

Chapter One

Diamond rolled in a patch of her favorite grass, the South Florida sunshine warming her belly. Spreading her paw wide over a four-leaf clover, she grabbed it with her extra finger. A polydactyl cat, she enjoyed her special paws.

A child's strangled screams rent the air, nearly deafening her, chilling her soul. Hideous grunts mortified her, freezing her blood. Then she smelled it. Mildew and death. The neighborhood fiend had returned, mercilessly hunting new prey.

Alarm flooding her, she crept closer to the sound, her heart in her throat. The terrified cries belonged to the child who lived next door, the one who liked to cuddle her until she almost suffocated.

She didn't know what a cat could do to thwart a ravenous alligator, but she couldn't stand by and let the ogre hurt the little boy.

Screeching as loudly as she could, she called for reinforcements, hoping it wasn't already too late. As long as the child screamed, he was still alive. As long as there was life, hope remained, however slim.

Streaking across the lawn, she leaped to the top of the fence, bounded down, and stared at the horrifying scene, her fur standing on end. The lethal creature chased the child at an amazing speed. It was much more agile than a bulky leathery being had any right to be. Huge jaws opened wide, and Diamond knew the young boy had no defense against its filthy, razor-sharp teeth. The gigantic creature would swallow him whole. The child's only chance was if someone took his place — now. The seconds of his life ticked away.

No one else was in sight, human or animal. Where was that pesty dog Napoleon when she needed him? He never missed an opportunity to make her life miserable, but at least he could help her in a dire emergency. Eddie must have put him inside.

Terror engulfed her. Praying she would be reincarnated and elevated in her next life, Diamond darted between the boy and the monster, her claws sharp and ready to shred his soulless eyes. "Fight someone who can fight back, creepazoid." Baring her fangs, her back arched, and her ears flattened against her head.

"An appetizer before the main course," the disgusting creature taunted her, thrashing his long tail.

"Run!" she screamed to the catatonic kid, frustrated that he couldn't understand her. *Why, oh why, couldn't humans understand her?* She understood them.

Mustering her courage, adrenaline surged through her body. She screeched to distract the monster, her reflection in its black, soulless eyes valiant. Her tail pointed skyward stiffly. Her white fur bristled on her arched back. Her normally sunny eyes glittered almost as dark as the gator's.

Snarling, her claws fully extended, her fangs ready, she swiped the monster's long snout as she hissed, "Leave him alone!"

Long, deep scars engraved the leathery snout. With a pained grunt, the fiend whirled around on her, its huge maw snapping. Never had she seen such an enormously horrifying mouth. The beast could almost swallow the boy whole. He'd surely ingest her in one gulp.

Gnashing teeth ripped her flesh apart, and excruciating pain flooded her. Relief cut through the agonizing pain when the child's father ran up and pulled his son to safety and then tried to pry her from the creature's jaws. Wanting to be brave, she tried not to cry, but to no avail. Never had she dreamed such excruciating pain could exist. Finally, blessedly, darkness descended.

* * * * *

"You did well, my precious Diamond. Your noble sacrifice saved the child." The most beautiful honeyed voice Diamond had ever heard wrapped her in silk.

She opened one eye and peered in the direction of the intoxicating voice. Her blurry vision slowly cleared. The loveliest human she had ever seen smiled serenely at her. The angelic being seemed to be floating on white fluffy clouds. Spears of sunlight pierced her transparent, sparkling body. Raven locks curled over her shoulders to her slender waist.

Diamond's memory returned in bits and pieces. Flashes of the young child terrified, trying to escape from a monster, stabbed her. Then she saw a huge throat cavity and rows of horrific teeth. Shuddering, she squeezed her eyes shut against the frightening images that bombarded her.

"Don't be scared, little one. You're safe here."

Here?

Diamond chanced another glance at her airy surroundings and realized she, too, floated on mere wisps of air. Startled, she clawed for purchase, her paws slicing invisible air. Oxygen filled her lungs but she couldn't exhale. Gasping, she asked the woman, "Where is *here*?"

"You're in Heaven, my pet. I'm called Venus, Goddess of Love. I brought you here." A sunny smile curved the goddess's beautiful lips and lit her exquisite features.

"Heaven?"

Where were all the golden mice? The golden goblets of fresh milk? The raw meat cut into bite-sized chunks?

Then a much more poignant thought struck her full in the chest, making her heart ache unbearably. "I'll never see my master Eddie again? But he'll be distraught! What will he do without me? Who will guard his house? Who will he cuddle up to at night?"

"A truly noble soul." Venus beamed satisfaction upon her. "Your concern is still with your master."

Diamond wasn't sure exactly how noble her feelings were in regards to her master, so she veiled her eyes from Venus' discerning gaze. She'd wished nightly that she could be in his bed, in his arms in a totally different manner—that she could be a human female...

Venus scooped her up in her silky arms and played with Diamond's extra finger. She whispered in her ear, her breath warm and ticklish, "I can read your thoughts."

Impossible!

Diamond's eyes widened. She curled her paw around the woman's finger. Her whiskers twitched as her tail wrapped around her body. Never before could a human read her mind. Of course, she had never been able to converse in human before, either. This Heaven was the strangest place she'd ever seen, and that included all the moving pictures she'd watched in that little box in Eddie's living room that transported her to faraway destinations.

Venus said, "Heaven's beyond your dearest dreams. We're in the reception area. But I wonder...it wasn't your time to die. You were due several more years on Earth."

Diamond sucked in her breath. Did that mean the goddess might send her back to her master? *How wonderful.*

Venus rubbed behind her ears, making her purr. "Um...can I send you back?" The beauty stared into space, her gaze cloudy.

Diamond held her breath hoping with all her soul. *Please!* She wanted to see Eddie so badly she ached.

After several long moments Venus looked down at her. "Would you like to return to Earth as a human?"

Diamond blinked. She'd forever hoped she could be a human female so she could love Eddie, but she hadn't dared dream her fantasy could ever become reality. She'd have jumped into an alligator's maw sooner if she'd known. "I would love it and be eternally grateful. But where will I live?"

"Wherever you want to live, of course. As a human, you'll have the freedom to choose for yourself." A soft breeze swished Venus' full skirts about her legs.

"With Eddie?" Diamond's heart beat a suffocating drumbeat at the idea of living with Eddie as a human female.

The goddess brushed stray wisps of dark hair away from her eyes. "That I cannot guarantee. But I can return you to his neighborhood, and then you must make your own way. Hurry and decide—I have another pressing mission awaiting my attention."

"Yes!" Diamond leapt for joy. Any chance was better than none. She missed Eddie so very much, she could barely breathe.

"Find a way to make Eddie love you, little one. Be your sweet, gentle spirit, and he'll see what a treasure you are. Do you still want me to change you into a human? Say the word."

"Yes, please! I'll use all my wiles to make Eddie fall in love with me. I'll rub his head and curl up on his lap. I'll lick him all over. I'll hunt for him. My master won't be able to resist."

A slight frown tugged at Venus' lips, marring her flawless face. "Word of warning, my Diamond. Once I transform you, you'll be human on the outside and you'll have many human traits, but your heart and soul will always be part feline. If you want to fit in and take your new rightful place, you must guard against your old nature. In time, it will get easier, but you have much to learn. The human world is a complex one."

Diamond's hopes crashed. "You don't think I can adjust? But I've lived with humans my entire life. I know humans so well." She had paid much more attention to humans than her siblings who had thought her obsession with her master and his kind demented.

"Yet you speak of hunting for food and you call him 'my master'. Humans rarely hunt, especially not today's females…"

How backwards!

"Females are born to hunt." It was her duty to catch food for her family.

The raven-haired goddess shook her head. "Not in the human world. Human females open boxes and cans to eat, instead of gathering food. They order in food from restaurants. You have much to learn." Venus tapped her finger against her lips and paced in front of Diamond. "Perhaps I was too hasty with my reward. Perhaps cats cannot fit into the human world. You won't even know how to read, or write...or cook." Venus nibbled her lip and knelt down by Diamond's side.

No! She couldn't change her mind now.

Alarm slamming through Diamond, she rose on her haunches to pat Venus' cheek with a gentle paw. "You can't promise me the moon and stars and then yank it away from me thus. I know I can learn. Please give me a chance. No one could love my master the way I do."

"And you won't blame me if everything isn't perfect? If Eddie does not fall desperately, irrevocably in love with you? If you don't find the human world as much to your liking as you dream?" Indecision flickered across Venus' worried eyes.

Diamond held up her paw somberly. "I shall not hold anything against you, your grace. I will be grateful for a second chance at life, to merely be with my master, whether he chooses me as his true mate or not."

Indecision flickered across Venus' darkened eyes. "Your emotions will intensify. Your heart will swell and be capable of holding much more ache than you ever imagined."

"I'm sure. Please make me a woman. I am anxious to see how I shall look."

An indulgent smile lit the goddess's face. "You won't miss your exquisite fur?"

Diamond shook her head emphatically. "It will be easier to keep myself clean, and I won't be as warm in the hot time of year."

"You won't miss your whiskers?"

"I won't try to squeeze under beds and into tight places." She wouldn't need to.

"You won't miss your agility? You won't be able to run as fast or jump as high."

"But I'll be able to soar to the heights of love and acquire knowledge beyond that of any other cat since the inception of the universe."

Venus' lips curved upward at that, and she nodded approvingly. Then she sobered again. "You won't have nine lives anymore."

"Did I have nine lives when the alligator swallowed me? I'm here, aren't I?"

"Yes, my little Diamond. You have a point." The goddess tapped her finger against her curving lower lip. "I must make a condition of my own. I will give you six months in which to win the love of a human male. If in that time, you fail, you shall revert to your former self and live out the rest of your days as a cat. Do you agree to my terms?"

Oh, yes!

Diamond could find love in six human months. After all that was the equivalent of three and a half years in feline time. Determined to make Eddie fall in love with her, she nodded. If he didn't, what good would it do to remain human anyway? Diamond licked her lips, her whiskers twitching eagerly. "I agree. How soon can I return?"

"Why not now?" Venus set the cat gently on her paws, backed away a few steps and tapped her head with a golden scepter. Radiant light shot forth, bathing Diamond in its luminescence.

Wild anticipation shot through her, starting at her heart and coiling to the tip of her tail, which stood straight up. "Will I still have white fur?"

"Hair, Diamond. You'll have to watch each word that rolls off your tongue lest you give yourself away. Humans do not have fur. You will have hair now, and yes, it will be a white blonde. I'm not changing your essence. Your eyes will still be amber as well. See for yourself."

Strange sensations quivered down Diamond's spine, jolting her heart. Her paws mutated, bulged, and pulsed. The fur shrunk and simply disappeared before her amazed eyes leaving smooth, naked pink flesh. Her claws retracted and then her toes elongated into delicate fingers and human toes. She flexed them, and they had much more agility than her paws ever had.

She spun around when her tail began to throb. It pulled into her body as her torso stretched and twisted into new shapes. Her legs divided, the back ones growing long and curvy, the front sprouting as her toes had only seconds before. Then her teats flattened except for two that rounded into lush, melon-shaped orbs. She blinked down at her well-endowed, nude self, and covered the white blonde curls between her legs with her new hand.

"You are now remade in my image." Venus' glowing smile bathed her. The goddess circled her, and regarded her closely. "I must say you make a gorgeous woman."

How wonderful!

Pleased, a large smile tugged at Diamond's lips. She curtsied deeply in homage.

A man's shape shimmered into focus beside Venus. Transparent like the woman, sunlight showered through him. He too wore a white sheet draped around him and a grape leaf vine encircled his hair, silvery as the moonlight. Unlike the beautiful goddess, a scowl marred his perfect features. "What is taking so long, Vee? Father's been searching every inch of Heaven for you."

Sighing, Venus said, "It seems I'm being summoned, so it's time for you to go back." The goddess kissed her cheek and regarded her with much love. "Good luck. Be happy. And be careful. Remember, you only have six months to make Eddie fall in love with you."

Diamond nodded and gulped, pushing away the niggling doubt that six months didn't give her enough time. In human time, it wasn't very long, or so she'd heard him say. "I'll do everything in my power to make Eddie fall in love with me."

How she longed for him to hold her and make her quiver with long, soul-shattering kisses, to be under his bewitchment.

"You have a rare soul. I won't regret giving you this chance." The beauty's inner glow radiated outward, bathing Diamond in her warmth.

"I'll make you proud of me." Her heart swelling with anticipation and joy, she tingled all over. Soon she would be with Eddie and he would love her as she loved him.

"Come, sister," Venus' brother said, his voice ringing with annoyance. "Father's growing impatient. You know he thinks you touched in the head to turn felines into people and people into toads. He's still raging about the time you turned that prince into a frog, and he blabbered about his exploits to that loose-lipped bard who spread it across the land."

Venus rolled her eyes and slanted a naughty smile Diamond's way. "Father should get over it already. That was nigh on a millennium ago. And I turned that blabbermouth into a dragon so he could really let out his hot air."

The young man, who looked long on wisdom and short on temper, peered up at the dimming sun. "Time grows short. Do what you must, but do not include me in your escapades. I do not need Father's wrath on my head. His memory is eternal."

"He should be so long on forgiveness. A thousand years is too long to hold a grudge. No wonder he has such terrible heartburn." Venus waved her hand with a flourish, and a looking glass hovered before her nose. "See how beautiful you look as a human."

Diamond peered closely at flawless alabaster flesh, rosy cheeks the color of cherry blossoms, and lush lips, pink like the petunias in Eddie's garden. True to Venus' word, her *hair* was white. Not ivory as her fur had been, but a slightly more golden, human shade. All in all, she made a stunning human. "I approve." Hopefully Eddie would, too.

"When I count to three, you'll appear back on Earth. Good luck. May love bloom between you." The goddess hugged her and her sweet-smelling breath tickled Diamond's sleek neck.

Venus stepped back and winked as a dreamy smile curved her lips. "Remember, humans cook their meat and eat it with forks. They don't consume heads or eyes. And they drink their liquids, not lap them with their tongues."

Diamond couldn't stop the wistful smile from curving her lips. Soon, she would take on Eddie on an even level.

The goddess touched Diamond with the wand again, chanting, "One. Two. Three."

Chapter Two

Eddie wiped the dirt from his hands down his jeans. His heart aching, he offered a solemn prayer to honor his beloved cat. His faithful dog Napoleon sat by his side. A rare Hemmingway-type cat, his Diamond had been a great model and an even more wonderful pet. The small statue which he had placed in her favorite lounging place under the ficus tree would memorialize her and hold her in his heart forever. The one and only magazine cover he'd sold had been of her, so that would now serve as a wonderful tribute. He didn't know if he had the heart to submit the final pictures of her for publication. He'd probably just hang them in his private gallery.

Napoleon yipped excitedly, and bounded for the back of the yard. He leaped at the chain-link fence, his stubby tail wagging, and he exuded a happiness Eddie wished he could feel again.

Eddie watched him for a few minutes and when he didn't see anything, he finished the service. Probably more ducks swimming down the canal. It didn't take much to excite a dog.

As he turned to go back into the house and clean up, Napoleon began to bark in earnest. Curious, Eddie ambled to the back of the yard to check out what the commotion was about. Movement alongside the water's edge caught his attention, and he proceeded with caution, even though he was inside his fenced yard. Since the recent incident in which he had lost his Diamond, he watched the canal very closely in case he could prevent another tragedy.

What the hell?

Blinking, he did a double take. He could swear a naked woman strolled alongside the bank.

Rocking back on his haunches, his pulse leapt. It was everything he could do to bite back a whistle of awe. A lot of strange things had been happening in his quiet, backwater neighborhood lately, but he still couldn't believe his eyes. He had to be dreaming.

But, oh, what a vision! If he was dreaming, he never wanted to wake up. Waist-length sun-kissed golden hair tickled the mirage's shapely hips. The silky curtain hid her body one step, and then swung back to reveal lush breasts with rose-tipped nipples the next. Golden sparks shot from her hair with every sway of her hips.

He had to be hallucinating. He'd been slaving too long under the sizzling south Florida sun. It must have baked his addled brain. He'd wasted months searching for a model, and now he imagined that this gift had dropped out of heaven just for his personal gain? He was definitely losing it!

Still, he'd be a fool to let this vision walk away without taking a shot. He had about given up on finding the right woman to model the new swimsuit line he'd been commissioned to photograph. "Thank you, God," he murmured under his breath, putting his sorrow on the back burner until he was better able to deal with it.

Slowly, the fog clouding his brain lifted. If anyone else spied this naked nymph in a suburban neighborhood, they would call the police. He happened to think the naked woman was *extremely* decent, but knew the cops wouldn't agree. The buffoons would haul her downtown, book her for indecent exposure, and frighten the wits out of her.

Worse, it wasn't safe for a woman to walk around naked in Fort Lauderdale, not even in this normally sleepy little burg. Nor was this canal very safe to hang about. Only the other day, the unthinkable had almost happened when an alligator had risen from its midst and threatened the neighbor boy. In the process, the monster had murdered his pet instead, and he still ached for the sweet little cat that used to purr like a motorboat, warming his heart. He even missed the way she used to rub against his ankles when she vied with Napoleon for his food.

Making up his mind to make her acquaintance and play a little knight in shining armor, he followed her. "You look a little lost, Lady Godiva. Need some help?"

An angelic smile crossed the nymph's lips, warring with questions in her eyes. "Lady Godiva?"

She'd never heard of Lady Godiva? What planet had she come from? "You really shouldn't traipse around here like that."

Lady Godiva glanced down at her nude form and blushed prettily. "I don't have any clothes."

He gulped, and his hands grew clammy. How could someone not have any clothing? He shrugged out of his shirt, draped it over her, and buttoned it. His shirttails barely fell to the juncture of her legs. Her nipples stood out against the soft cotton making this outfit nearly more erotic than her complete nudity.

At such close distance, her spellbinding scent wafted around him. Just a hint of saltwater clung to her. Maybe she was a mermaid that had swum inland by mistake. That made about as much sense as anything else

A mermaid? He was well and truly losing it. He shook himself mentally, trying to erase impossible lusty fantasies from his mind.

"Thank you." When the ravishing beauty licked her full lips, beaming up at him, his heart melted and his cock stood at full staff. She raised wide amber eyes to him, so beautiful he could drown in them. "I don't know."

Bizarre. She was the most beautiful woman he'd ever seen, but she was also the strangest. "You don't know if I can help you?"

She shook her head slowly, catching sunbeams in her flaxen hair. Awe twinkled in her eyes when she gazed about as if she'd never seen such sights before. He was back to leaning toward the alien theory. "It looks so small."

Small? Compared to what? Pine trees grazed the sky in his backyard as sun dappled the grass through their mossy shade. "This is Fort Lauderdale." Part of the huge metropolis of Miami-Fort Lauderdale, it was not exactly a small town.

"It's nice."

Definitely bizarre. If they stayed out here much longer, someone was bound to call the police. Not an option. "Do you live around here?"

Sadness fluttered about Lady Godiva's beautiful full lips. "In another lifetime."

Now she was reincarnated? "Are you visiting someone in the neighborhood? How about I escort you home?" Anxiety weighed heavily on his mind. He couldn't say why, but this woman raised his protective instincts. Maybe because she looked so innocent, so guileless.

She tucked her glorious hair behind her ear, her smile fading into a grim line. "I don't have any place to go. There's nowhere to take me."

"When's the last time you ate?" He swore under his breath that this lovely woman seemed to be on her own.

Her brow furrowed and she seemed to look inward. "I don't remember when. Maybe yesterday?"

His own stomach growled in sympathy. This damsel in distress was definitely in need of rescuing, not his usual line of work. "It's amazing you can still stand."

Afraid she would recoil, he held out his hand to her slowly. Pleased when she put her warm, small, and delicate hand in his trustingly, he showered her with his smile. Electric currents shot up his arm. "Come with me. Let's get some food into you before you collapse. We need to let your family know where you are before they call out the police." He took her arm and guided her to his house.

Sadness spreading across her exquisite features, she shook her head and his shirt rose alarmingly. "I don't have any family left."

Embarrassed, albeit fascinated, he looked away. She had to have someone. "Friends?"

"No one."

Maybe she had amnesia. He was running out of plausible theories. This seemed the most logical out of any of them he'd considered so far. He couldn't keep calling her Lady Godiva. "What's your name? Do you have identification?" The moment the words sprung off his lips, he rolled his eyes at his stupidity. *Moron!* Where could a naked woman hide identification?

"I'm called Dia..." She paused, a look of horror flitting across her face.

"Diana?" he puzzled the partial name together and hazarded a guess, wondering why the look of terror? Suspicions ate at him. Something didn't add up.

Immediately she brightened, the radiance of her smile stealing his breath. "Yes. It's Diana."

The beautiful, elegant name suited her. He closed the sliding glass door behind her and locked it. Then he pulled the vertical blinds across the window lest nosy neighbors peer into his domain. The people living in the apartments across the canal could spy straight into his living room if they had a mind to, and he wasn't in a mood to parade his business in front of anybody. "What's your last name?"

Consternation twisted her exquisite features again, wrenching his heart, against his better judgment. After a drawn out pause, her eyes downcast, she admitted, "Venus."

Why was she so hesitant to give her last name? Should he contact the authorities for help? He'd think about it a while. Meanwhile, he didn't see the harm in filling her with a little food. "I'm not exactly Emeril Lagasse, but I can whip up something edible. Tuna or chicken okay?"

Light leapt in her eyes and her stomach growled. "I adore fish and meat. They're my favorite."

Okay. He'd been told that by a lot of dates. The more Lady Godiva chattered, the weirder she sounded. "Tuna sandwiches, it is." He paused at the door, his hand curved around the frame. Extending his free hand to her, he introduced himself. "By the way, I'm Eddie."

"Thank you, Eddie." When she took his hand, his heart flipped over. A beautiful smile dawned over her face when she caressed his name and his knees went so weak he had to lean against the wall.

He had to get a grip. This wasn't the time to think about himself and the troubling sensations this woman evoked. Diana needed help. He made the sandwiches and handed her a plate. Then he poured two glasses of iced tea and carried them to the kitchen table and claimed the chair beside her.

She sniffed the drink, and wrinkled her nose. She proceeded to push the glass away from her and ignore it.

He took the hint. "Would you prefer soda or juice to drink?"

Diana rewarded him with a sunny smile. "I'd love some milk, if you have it. If not, water would be good."

Eddie scraped his chair back and made his way to the fridge. "One long tall glass of milk coming right up." He poured it into a glass and set it before her.

An appreciative smile lit her face, and she lifted the glass to her lips. Instead of sipping it, she lapped at it with her tongue.

Odder and odder. He had to tear his gaze away from his guest.

But he wasn't quick enough and when she caught his stare, her eyes widened, and the color drained from her cheeks. Her tongue froze in mid-lap, and she stared cross-eyed at the milk before taking a careful sip.

What had he just witnessed? Did it hold any special significance? "Is there anywhere I can take you? Anything I can do to help?"

She traced her fingertip around the rim of her glass, and seemed to look inward. "I don't know."

Either she couldn't remember or she didn't want him to know. It was time to involve the authorities. "I'm going to call the police and they can help find your people."

Alarm blazed in her eyes, and she yelled, "No! Please don't."

Her reaction startled him. He wanted to help her, not traumatize her. Neither did he want to harbor a fugitive, not that he could envision such a sweet woman being a dangerous criminal. "Are you in some kind of trouble with the law?"

"No, I promise."

"Then what's the problem? I can't just send you out on the street with nowhere to go. I could take you to a homeless shelter and they can help you find a job and a place to live." It didn't sound like much of a solution, but he was running out of options and the social workers who staffed the homes would be far better equipped to help her.

A sorrowful expression pinched her face, to be chased away by one of hope and longing. "Couldn't I stay here with you?"

He blinked. She wanted to stay with him? What was he supposed to do with her? How could he help her? Then an outlandish, perhaps brilliant thought struck him. He really needed a model, and she really needed a source of income. "Have you ever modeled?"

"Modeled?" She tilted her head and twitched her nose in a way that fascinated him. She really had an oddly, but beautifully expressive face that would translate well onto film. And he knew without a doubt that she had a dynamite figure just made to model swimsuits.

Patiently he explained, "Modeling is when someone takes pictures of you for an advertisement."

To his relief, she nodded. "I've had my picture taken a lot. My mast—friend used to take a lot of pictures of me. He said the camera loved me."

"Where can we find your friend? Do you have his phone number and address?" Hope flared in his gut. Finally they were getting somewhere.

"No…" A shutter seemed to come down over her face and she pursed her lips.

"What's your friend's name?"

A deer-in-the-headlights look flickered across her eyes and she tensed for several seconds. Although he wasn't a detective and had no law enforcement training, her reaction didn't strike him as someone who didn't remember. Rather, she didn't appear to want him to discover a secret. Could she be frightened of this so-called friend? If so, he didn't want to push her. Instead, he'd give her a little space and time. He supposed it wouldn't hurt him to let her stay a few days.

Backtracking, he dropped the matter of the friend. "I need a model and you need a job. How about it? Are you willing to give it a go? I have an extra room where you can crash until you get on your feet." He hoped he wouldn't regret his impulsive offer. He'd do some quiet checking up on her so as not to alarm her. Hopefully, she'd start to trust him and open up to him.

Relief flooded her eyes and the tension visibly ebbed out of her. A proud smile curved her lips. "I always land on my feet."

Now it was his turn to feel relief. "Glad to hear it."

* * * * *

Eddie led Diana back to the living room and motioned for her to sit on the couch. "You have the perfect face and figure to launch the line of swimsuits I'm photographing. I guarantee we'll be a success together. Interested?"

"Yes!" She couldn't bite back her enthusiasm, she was so excited, and yet, she wondered how she'd displeased him that he had practically pushed her out. She tried to tamp down her soaring spirit a few notches. It wasn't quite a marriage proposal, but at least she'd be near him. "When do we start?"

"Whoa! We haven't even talked terms. You know, wages...living arrangements." Skepticism glinted in his dark eyes and his Adam's apple bobbed in his throat. "Aren't you interested?"

Actually, she couldn't care less about something called *wages*. As long as she could live in her home, with her master, have food and shelter, she was satisfied, ecstatic even. But Eddie's attitude alerted her that he expected her to care and found it peculiar that she had been so eager to accept his offer without knowing such pertinent details.

"Oh, of course," she said, trying to cover her obviously grievous slip. Cuticles annoyed her fingers, especially when she grew nervous, and she pushed at them as she tried to get her nerves under control. "My mission in life is to please you."

The pulse in the base of Eddie's neck raced faster and he shifted in his seat as if uncomfortable as he stared at her. "If you really mean that, you may be too good to be true."

"Oh, I do! I am!" Eager to please, she scooted forward and sat ramrod straight. "I'd love to model swimsuits." Whatever they were.

Eddie's unblinking gaze smoldered, making her flesh flame. "You'll look like dynamite."

She hoped that was good. "Thank you! Thank you!" It was her turn to exhale in relief. The pent-up breath she'd been holding in whooshed out. *Yes, I'm home!*

"Follow me. I'll show you to your room." Eddie hitched up his slacks and rose to his full height.

Excitement thrummed through her veins. Her very own room! She sped upstairs to the guest bedroom, stood in the middle and felt like hugging herself so much joy flooded her. An entire room of her own! No more getting kicked off the bed, tossed off the couch, or put out the door when she wanted to nap. Heaven!

Eddie leaned against the doorjamb, his arms crossed over his chest. The frown was back and she lamented that he had glowered more today at her than in the past three years. "How do you know this is the room I was going to put you in?"

She turned to face him and mustered a pleasant smile. Rats! She was making too many mistakes and he would start to suspect something wasn't right about her and she couldn't afford that. More than anything in the world, she wanted to stay with him. She'd have to be a lot more careful. "Be-because this is the only spare bedroom."

"How did you know that? Or that it was upstairs?"

"Your personal things are in the other bedroom. And there's no personal things in this room." Spartan, the room contained empty bookshelves, a plain bedspread, and an empty closet. No knickknacks littered the shelves and countertops, just perfect to curl up on. No books lay scattered about. It didn't look lived in. Not even a trace of her beautiful fur remained on the bed. The other room contained all his equipment and photographs, many of her former self. She hadn't lied when she told him she'd been photographed often. Eddie's camera had adored her and her picture had even graced the cover of a cat magazine once.

"*Mi casa es su casa.*"

She'd never heard him say that before and hadn't heard it come out of that TV box he liked to watch, either. She must have given him a blank stare at the incomprehensible words, for he said, "My house is your house."

Just as before. Their house. His declaration sounded absolutely wonderful, like catnip.

A yawn stole over her, which she tried to stifle with her hand quite ineffectually. What she wouldn't give to curl up on a nice soft cushion and give herself a languorous tongue bath. She eyed the bed longingly.

Eddie nodded at her yawn and said, "You look like you need some rest. Feel free to take a nap."

Great! She could handle this. "That sounds heavenly." She lowered herself to the bed and curled up beside the pillow.

Eddie's brows drew into a single line and he ambled over to her. Bending low, he turned down the bedding. "You'll be more comfortable beneath the sheets."

Diana wanted to flatten her ears back at yet another mistake, but the cartilage wouldn't budge, frustrating her. She'd seen Eddie asleep countless times to know that humans usually crawled inside the bed and rested their heads on a pillow. Venus had warned her to be careful, and she must be disappointing her, if she was watching. Once she rested up and her head was clear again, she'd do a better job. She had to! She couldn't allow Venus to send her back, away from Eddie.

If she just concentrated hard enough, was observant enough, she could pull this off, make Venus proud of her and most importantly, win Eddie's love. She'd have to watch that television box a lot to study human ways, though if she had any hope of succeeding. She wished she'd paid closer attention to it before. But her ears had been more sensitive in her former life, and it had emitted sounds that made them ache. With decreased hearing, hopefully it wouldn't be a problem anymore.

Chapter Three

The dog howled, startling her awake. Diana leapt off the bed, looking for her old nemesis, but he must be downstairs. Bright morning light streamed through the window, spotlighting her. Obviously, she wasn't nocturnal anymore. Had Eddie tried to wake her up? Judging by the height of the sun, several hours had passed.

Stretching, she lifted her arms high above her head and worked the kinks out of her shoulders. Curling up in a ball hadn't been the best idea since her reincarnation due to her different bone structure. Humans weren't as agile as cats. Pity. She made a note of that for future reference, not happy at how long her list of things to remember was growing. Would she ever learn everything she needed to know?

Her stomach growling, she made her way to the kitchen and hunted through the cabinets for food, knowing the fresh meat and fish were stored in the chilly box. She'd tried to climb in after the delicious smells once and had nearly died when Eddie had closed the door, trapping her inside. Luckily he had rescued her before she became a catsicle. But it still gave her the chills although she told herself she was too large to fit inside the tiny compartment any longer, so there was no danger of her being trapped.

She took out a few cans and boxes depicting pretty pictures that made her mouth water. Fish in small tins reminded her of her favorite moist cat food and made her stomach rumble. Luscious, creamy milk and beautiful, yellow cheese that made her want to purr. The question was how could she make it attractive and edible for the humans to eat? As she recalled, Eddie usually mixed the food together in those containers that looked like a dream-sized cat food dish, so she searched for those and found a large one. Pleased, she ripped open the milk and cheese with her teeth, spilling it onto the countertop and floor. Frustration settled in when she couldn't figure out how to open the uncooperative tin can and she suppressed a moan. Fingernails didn't work. Not even teeth. How she missed her fangs!

Confounded, she peered at the mechanical gadgets in the kitchen wondering if one of them would puncture it. She couldn't understand the scratchings on the cooking machine or the other items on the counter. Intimidated, she stared at them several minutes, pondering how to make them work. Hunger pangs making her stomach ache, she pounded the can against the counter, making a horrific racket.

"Whoa! Looks like that milk and cheese attacked you." His unruly hair still damp from the shower, his shirttails flopping behind him, Eddie swaggered into the room, eying the mess she had made. Soap and cologne perfumed his body curling around her nostrils. She sniffed appreciatively, wanting to wrap herself up in the wonderful scents, or better yet, next to the warm man.

First things first. She held up the uncooperative can, eying it cross-eyed. "How do I open this?"'

Eddie scratched his head and looked around. "Aha! The can opener's hiding behind the canisters. Here's the scoundrel." He reached behind some large clear sealed bowls containing grains and white powders and pulled out a rectangular metal box. She watched raptly as he opened the can, making mental notes for future reference.

"Thank you." When he handed the open can to her their fingertips grazed one another. Sparks flew and she jerked her hand away. As pleasing as it had been, his touch had never done this to her before. These human sensations threatened to overwhelm her.

"Guess it would help if I show you all my hiding places and how the oven works." He proceeded to take out the paper towels and helped her wipe up the milky mess. Then he explained how to operate the stove and gave her a tour of the cabinets. "I'll leave you to it. No woman wants a man underfoot in the kitchen."

The term "underfoot" elicited memories of when she used to brush against his legs whenever he prepared food. She could totally stand to reverse their roles and have him rub against her.

* * * * *

The dog began barking like a maniac.

Almost simultaneously, Eddie smelled smoke, and started to cough. Maybe the next door neighbors were grilling out again. They favored the hickory-flavored shish kebobs and big juicy steaks that made his mouth water. Napoleon's too, obviously. It had been too long since he'd grilled out. Now that he had a houseguest, he'd have to fire up the grill and thaw a couple succulent steaks.

The smell grew stronger in the den where he worked at his computer desk, and he frowned. It wasn't coming from outside. Pushing the chair back, he rose to his feet and followed the smell. When Diana coughed heavily and the dogs barking grew more frantic, his heart lurched. Just as he reached the hallway, he spied wisps of smoke floating along the ceiling.

Shit!

"Diana! Where are you?"

"Kitchen. Help!" Diana's coughing worsened.

Adrenaline burst in his veins kicking him into high gear. His gut clenching, he ran toward the kitchen. Flames danced merrily in the kitchen, consuming his stove and the nearby cabinet. Soot clung to the walls and cabinetry.

The damned flames seemed to be alive and tried to grab the woman who jumped back and forth, gagging on the smoke. To make matters worse, the crazy dog leapt around crazily.

Shit! His house was on fire.

"Get back and get the dog outside." Gritting his teeth, Eddie grabbed the fire extinguisher from the wall, and doused the flames. He shook his head, surveying the damage.

What a mess.

Diana trudged back with a somber expression making her complexion gray. Trembling, her amber eyes murky, she stared at the mess. "I'm sorry. I thought that yellow water would put out the fire, not make it larger."

Massaging the kinks from the back of his neck, he sighed. She could have been killed. She was damned lucky the fire hadn't exploded in her pretty face. At least there weren't any visible burns. The kitchen could be repaired. This would give him an excuse to replace the ugly mustard-colored cabinets. "You okay? You didn't get burned did you?"

She covered her mouth with her hand and coughed. Her eyes were so wide they took up almost half her face. "No. No burns. I'm just a little shaky. I didn't know that could happen."

"I've got this handled. Why don't you go wash up?"

Covered in grime, soot clinging to her hair, she nodded. "Good idea." She scampered up the stairs and soon footsteps sounded overhead.

As Eddie took inventory of the damage, the shower's running water pounded the floor overhead reminding him how his tight schedule wouldn't easily permit him to waste a day in such a mundane pursuit as hunting for a new stove and counters. He'd worry about the house later. First he had to earn the means to finance the repairs. His first priority was to outfit and photograph his new model, a beauty who surely stood almost directly above him without a stitch of fabric covering her luscious curves.

Embers of a different type sparked in Eddie's groin. Inviting his new model to move in with him hadn't been one of his brighter ideas. He still had no idea where she came from or what kind of background she hid. He definitely couldn't go around with a hard-on every time she bathed. Hell, all she had to do was breathe and he became a giant hormone. How was he supposed to keep his mind on work?

The water stopped raining above and mere moments later, Diana traipsed down the stairs wearing his old T-shirt which swayed beguilingly about her thighs. Blushing prettily, Diana stared at him coquettishly through her absurdly long lashes. "I hope you don't mind that I borrowed this, but I didn't know what to put on."

Eddie gulped, his pulse ricocheting wildly. Her nipples strained enticingly against the fabric. Blood pumped furiously through his veins and the bulge in his pants swelled uncomfortably.

Nodding, her damp hair curling sweetly around her cheeks, Diana pivoted on her bare heel and headed away, her gently rounded bottom sashaying provocatively, making his mouth go bone dry. She slipped out the back door and murmured as she knelt on one knee to pet the dog, "You doing okay, Napoleon?"

Her words brought Eddie back to reality and he jerked his gaze away from her dangerous curves. Now she knew the dog's name? He hadn't introduced her to Napoleon. *Strange and stranger.* Had she been watching him before they met officially?

But he kept his thoughts private, tucking them away for future reference. He'd have to put his old college-buddy-cum-private-eye on her case to unravel some of her mysteries. The last thing he needed was trouble. Soon as he could get a private moment, he'd put in the call and get things moving.

"The least I can do is help clean up the mess." She ambled to the kitchen and swept up the mess. Bending over, she swept trash into the dustpan. Her sexy butt wriggled in the air and the back of the shirt hitched up, revealing her nudity.

What a tasty view. Perspiration broke out on his brow. Mesmerized, he couldn't take his gaze from her posterior. Was the siren trying to seduce him? Or perhaps she hadn't planned for him to see her feminine treasures. Still, she wasn't exactly being careful about hiding her wares from his avid gaze. Perhaps she wanted to see how hot she could make him. What kind of game was the hottie playing?

Hotter than the scorching beach sand, he yearned for respite. Oh, yeah. He'd never had a reaction to a woman like this before, had believed himself incapable of getting so turned on. He'd have to take a cold shower or get a lot of hand action before he could get some sleep. He snorted at the irony that a shower was responsible for getting him in this condition.

The object of his desire turned around, tossing a mischievous smile at him, stealing his breath. Mischievous mirth in her eyes made him wonder if she could read his mind, not that it would be extremely difficult to read right now. Hell, a woman would have to be blind and deaf to miss his reaction to her. His increased respiration and bulging arousal were dead giveaways.

He bent his knee to hide his obvious response from her, and tried to swallow his curses. What was he thinking, entertaining such erotic thoughts about a woman he'd just met? His own employee at that? One he knew nada about.

"I'll make this up to you," she said huskily, her honey tones glazing over him making him swallow hard, and trying his waning resolve. Was he imagining the silky seduction in her voice? Or did he yearn for it?

His muscles ached. Craving deliverance from this impossible position, he twisted around to rub his taut neck. "Don't worry about it. That's what insurance is for. The kitchen needed a new paint job and the cabinets were out of date."

She cozied up to his back. "Here, let me help you." Magic hands intended to soothe his neck and shoulders inflamed the wildfire already scorching him. Her breasts rubbed against his back, stealing his breath, and he sucked in a gulp of air. If he turned now, those bodacious breasts would rub against his chest, and his cock could rub against her stomach. He couldn't let it happen even though he craved it more than anything else.

He started to turn when pounding on the door broke through his haze. "Eddie?"

Glad of the last minute reprieve before he did something incredibly brainless, Eddie jerked away from the temptress and jumped to his feet. "Right here." He sped away, not completely sure he was thankful for the timely save.

Shawna, his assistant, waltzed into the house, swinging her briefcase. She stopped dead in her tracks when she spied Diana in the living room. Her eyes narrowed on the other woman as they raked over her state of undress. Her nostrils flaring, her gaze bounced to the charred kitchen and then back to him. "I've got the film you requested. Who is she?"

Eddie swore inwardly, took the case from her, and set it on the stairway, the only guaranteed dry spot in all of the downstairs. All he needed right now was a curious, pushy employee butting into his private affairs. "She's our new model—Diana. She'll be staying here until she gets on her feet."

"She's staying here—in this house—with you?" Disbelief warbled in Shawna's deadly quiet voice. Her chest heaved and her eyes narrowed, glittering dangerously.

"Yep." He wasn't about to defend what he did in his own house to his employee.

"What happened in here?" Shawna's brow rode high in her forehead as her heels clicked purposefully on the terrazzo tile as she peered around the destroyed kitchen.

"Cooking fire." He didn't feel like giving her a detailed explanation.

"Everybody okay?" As if she couldn't care less if the other woman was alive, Shawna's gaze raked coolly over Diana. It was a wonder she didn't turn into an icicle.

Seemingly unaffected by the arctic chill, his new model yawned and stretched by his side, the T-shirt lifting dangerously high, showing a long expanse of heart-stopping silky thigh. She was way too sensual for his peace of mind and Shawna looked like she wanted to scratch the blonde beauty to shreds.

He was well aware his assistant had designs on him, but he'd never taken her seriously. Now he sensed danger, as if he faced a trapped wild animal. "We're fine."

Uncomfortable with the situation, he beckoned Diana to join them. "Shawna, meet Diana, our new model. Diana, I'd like you to meet my assistant." Shawna detested the title secretary, feeling it demeaned her, so to keep the peace, he pacified her.

The bristling brunette faced off against him, firestorms raging in her eyes. "You hired a model without word one to me. Hmm...I could've sworn we were a team."

"I'm the boss." He'd never run management decisions past his assistant before and he'd be damned if he started now. He didn't need to start this precedent and he definitely didn't need a bigger headache.

Diana stepped forward, holding a slim hand out to the other woman in greeting. "I'm glad to meet you..."

Not surprisingly, Shawna ignored Diana's gesture and thrust a shaking finger at the blonde. "Why isn't she dressed?"

It was Eddie's turn to shoot back coolly, "Her clothes got messy so she's borrowing some of my things."

Shawna's brow tented. "She has no change of clothes?"

As ridiculous as it sounded to him, too, he wasn't about to let her know he agreed, which might send her straight to the authorities. He wasn't ready yet to bring his questions to them. Hopefully he'd never need to. "No."

"Let me get this straight—this woman crawled out from under a rock? And you're employing her?"

Diana's shoulders drooped and the smile slid off her formerly sunny face. "I didn't mean to cause trouble. I'll leave." She pushed past them and headed for the door, barefoot, clad in only his T-shirt.

He couldn't let her wander the streets in that preposterous condition, and he wasn't going to read about her in tomorrow's headlines. Blocking the doorway, he refused to let her escape; he told himself, for her safety. "Did I ask you to leave or say you were causing trouble?"

"N-no." Diana blinked back a tear from her watery eyes and it dangled precariously to her matted lashes.

Anger roiling in his gut, he turned and pinned his assistant with a lethal glare. "Thanks for the film, Shawna. That'll be all I need for now. I'll see you at the office tomorrow morning."

Her nose high in the air, Shawna huffed out of the house, and slammed the door behind her, shaking the thin walls. Not surprisingly, Napoleon barked furiously.

* * * * *

Later that evening after a tiring day, Eddie dimmed the downstairs lights in preparation to hit the sack. Diana must have stolen discreetly to her room when his attention had been diverted. With a sigh, he ambled upstairs and stretched out on his bed.

Just as he was closing his eyes, an angelic figure floated toward him. Hovering in the zone between waking and sleeping, he wasn't sure if the angel was for real or a vision. Silvery mist shimmered around her. Her scent cranked up his heat and sent his blood pounding furiously into his cock.

The exquisite creature nestled against his stomach. Then she leaned forward and began to massage his tense shoulders. She slid down his length, her T-shirt cottony soft against his engorged cock.

Positive he was dreaming, he moaned his pleasure and didn't stop his hand from exploring the luscious curves molding to his rock-hard length. When the siren moaned in chorus, he slid a hand under her shirt, pleased to find no restricting cloth denying access to her feminine charms. She wriggled against him deliciously when he slid a hand along her inner thigh.

His flesh flaming, he let his hand travel further north. He parted her swollen labia with his finger and eased it inside.

Hot and slick, she squirmed against him, moaning louder. Her nipples pebbled into hard little beads that rubbed against his chest through her covering. When her tongue flickered across his throat, it blazed a fiery erotic trail down his chest, making him quiver uncontrollably. Much more and he'd explode.

Quicksand pulled him under fast. Primitive longing to shoot his seed inside the luscious body assailed him. He flipped her over so that she molded perfectly to him. With a grunt, he stroked into the slick, heavenly vagina. Unable to resist her lure, he plunged to the hilt.

With hungry lips she suckled his male nipples as her hands explored his back. Reality had never been so wonderful and he hoped this dream would last forever.

Yearning to taste her, he rose high enough to yank her shirt over her head. He pulled a nipple into his mouth, elongating it. Sweet like nectar, he couldn't get enough. He wanted to pull the entire globe into his mouth, but she proffered much more than a mouthful. Suckling greedily, he pumped hard.

Her fingernails raked his back, but pain had never been so exquisite.

His lungs ready to burst, release came as he crushed the fantasy woman against him, flooding her with his seed. If only sex were half so hot in real life, he'd never climb out of bed.

Chapter Four

Diana almost climaxed with Eddie, but held back wanting to prolong the ecstasy. She reveled in the feel of his seed flooding her, spilling down her legs and coating her inner thighs.

Pushing him off her, she scrambled to her knees, presenting her backside to him. She wiggled it before his face, enticing him.

When he growled and drove his cock forcefully into her, ramming it almost to her womb, she screamed in ecstasy. His burning lust heated her. Stretching her as he slid in and out of her, he filled her, causing waves of pleasure to pour over her.

Nirvana!

Powerful as she knew he'd be, his hands created a feverish heat against her skin. Leaning over her, he cupped her breasts, kneading her nipples between his fingers. Licking her back, he pushed her flat to the bed, his cock nestling between her buttocks. When he probed a long finger into her anus, she gasped and ground against it greedily.

Her release came hot and heavy, triggering his own so that her fireworks illuminated her world.

Snuggling against his warmth, she purred against him. This was still her spot as it had always been and always would be. Soon enough, she'd win his heart. If he wasn't attracted to her, she couldn't arouse him to such a fevered pitch.

Immensely pleased, she patted herself where his seed resided. It was as it should be. No one could ever love him as she did. No one would take care of him and his children as she would.

Soon, his seed would fill her belly nightly. She would be such a fever in his blood, that he wouldn't be able to keep his hands or his tongue off her. His body would ache for her, and he would be all hers.

* * * * *

When he awoke late the next morning, Eddie felt more wonderful than he had in ages. Snippets of his dream replayed in his mind and he had trouble quelling the secretive smile that curved his lips. That had been some dream angel, made to his exact specifications.

He let Diana sleep in and headed to the office in his converted garage downstairs.

"You aren't seriously hiring that piece of fluff?" Shawna, who was already hard at work, greeted him in his office with her steno pad.

With a long, drawn out sigh, he sat down at his desk. "I can hire whomever I please. In case you forgot, I'm the boss." Although he had entertained second thoughts about Diana's suitability, he wouldn't give his haughty assistant the satisfaction of dismissing the woman from his employ.

Shawna's mouth gaped open. "I thought you valued my opinion."

"Did I ask for it?" Perhaps it was time to change assistants for a more amenable one. He'd put up with her attitude for far too long and she didn't seem to realize that her title of assistant meant that she assisted him, not dictated to him. He'd had enough and it was time to do something about it.

"Close the door and have a seat." When the brunette had settled into the chair opposite him, he folded his hands on top of the desk and leaned forward. "This arrangement isn't working out..."

All the blood drained from her face. Fury contorted her normally pretty features, erasing all traces of beauty as she leaned toward him. "Don't you think you're overreacting? You're letting your little head rule your big head."

"No. You were the one overreacting, Miss Moran." Fuming at his assistant's presumptions, he scribbled out a generous severance amount on a check, tore it from his book, and thrust it at her. "Clear out your desk now and kindly leave. Here's a check for one month's severance. If you want me to approve unemployment, you'll leave without a scene."

Shawna wrung her hands in her lap. Shadows flitted across her eyes. "I'm sorry, Eddie. I was wrong. I can't afford to lose my job. If I promise not to overstep my boundaries again, may I keep my position?"

He bit back a sigh. He wondered why everything she said and did annoyed him. As he wasn't a heartless monster, her plea tugged at him. He voided out the check and stuffed it in his pocket. "One more chance. But I expect you to treat our newest employee with the same respect and courtesy you do everyone else. Is that understood?"

Shawna nodded and bowed her head. "Yes, Eddie."

"Go on." He waved her away, not in the mood to take any more of her rebellion. And he added without looking up, "Close the door behind you, please."

She shut it softly, closing him into his silent room.

Unable to concentrate on work, his mind dwelled on his model. Ambling into the main part of the house, he hoped to find Diana awake.

Diana was eying the refrigerator hungrily when he found her.

"You up to earning your keep? Ready to do your first shoot on the beach?" He smiled at the vision of her in his shirt—and nothing else. "First, we'll stop by the mall and buy you a new wardrobe. Would you like that?"

"I'd love to," she said with a huskiness that wrapped itself around his swelling heart.

He could get used to her warm and husky voice. He couldn't wait to see her in a swimsuit. "My sister left a couple of her things in the spare closet last time she visited. She's about your size so they should fit you. Put one of her outfits on and then we'll pick up some bagels on the way."

Chapter Five

"Fabulous, doll. You're going to take us all the way to the top," Eddie said as Diana made love to his camera. He longed for her to make love to him and it was all he could do not to ravish her. A gift from heaven, she was just what he needed to kick-start his fledgling business. He prayed she would check out. But once the media met the ravishing beauty, lucrative financial offers would surely roll in. How could he keep her happy and in his employ?

Making a moue of her lips, the sex kitten writhed evocatively. The dusky areolas of her nipples strained against the silky fabric, making his mouth go dry. Uninhibited, proud of her body, she would make the perfect hot centerfold.

Much as she turned him on, his reaction became familiarly embarrassing as his jean cutoffs grew unbearably tight. Next time he was with her in public, he would wear loose-fitting pants. "Hold on a sec." He bit back a grimace and pulled an extra-large T-shirt over his head.

"All this clothing is so constricting." The siren pouted prettily, making his mouth go dry.

All what clothing? She was spilling out of her bandage of a suit.

For the life of him, he couldn't think of a plausible answer. On a personal level, he wished they could forego the annoying clothing, too. The sun would keep them warm and if it failed, he was sure Diana could find a way. But then he wouldn't have an income, thus, he couldn't eat. He thought quickly, self-preservation winning out by a touch. "We'd get a mighty sore sunburn if we didn't cover up."

She stroked her arm and then closed the gap between them and fondled him. "I'm not as furry as you. This exposed flesh isn't very practical."

Furry? She had a penchant to use strange descriptions that always made him do a double take. He glanced down inside his shirt to make sure he wasn't turning into a werewolf and satisfied himself that he wasn't that *furry.*

Her touch set him aflame and it was all he could do not to drop the camera he had retrieved from the soft bed of sand. Never had a light caress blasted his internal Richter scale off the chart. The hair on his arm seemed to have developed nerve endings and he yearned for more. Swallowing hard, he struggled to focus on getting this shoot finished while the light was still with them.

"Won't I get sunburned? I don't have a shirt on like you." She squinted up at the brutal sun beating down on them. It glowed brightly, shimmering.

"The sunscreen you put on earlier should protect you, but I can apply more to be on the safe side." Truth was, she wore long-lasting sunblock, but his fingers yearned to trace the contours of her luscious curves.

A frown tugged at the corners of her lips. "But if sunscreen will protect us, why do we need clothing?"

Her doggedness on the subject of nudity perplexed him, but charmingly so. Afraid he was falling under her spell, he murmured under his breath inaudibly, "Because I'd get arrested going around naked like this."

"It's against the law?" Her brow furrowed and her nose wrinkled. "Why?"

Damn but she had good hearing.

"Because it is." That clinched it. She was nuts. Or from Mars. Or maybe she had grown up in a nudist colony. Had she grown up in seclusion, unaccustomed to beaches? He would have to plan in advance for the next shoot and take her to Miami Beach or over to Barbados, where nude bathing was permitted.

She picked up the sunscreen and sauntered over to him, the sexy sashaying of her hips making him positively ravenous, but not for food. "Rub this on me?"

He accepted the tube in a daze, his fingers tingling to touch her. Once his fingers grazed her sizzling flesh, he was afraid he wouldn't be able to pull back. Not only would he screw up the shoot, he would cause a public disturbance. "Hold out your hands," he said, his voice raspy. Ignoring her pout, he squirted a generous supply of the cream into her palms.

It didn't take long to realize that merely having her self-apply the lotion wouldn't save his equilibrium. Brazenly, she slipped her hand inside her bikini bra and rubbed herself sensuously. In a stupor, he stared open-mouthed.

"Don't you want to photograph me?" Moving more sensually than could be legally allowed, she was being an unmerciful tease.

"More than anything, darlin'." Almost more than anything but the other thing was definitely illegal. Gulping, he aimed his camera at her and snapped several rolls of film as she made his groin harder than it had ever been. When she dipped her hand inside her bikini bottoms, stretching out the skimpy material so that he could see the shadow of her wiry curls, his palms grew sweaty. His grip slippery, he nearly dropped the camera. He'd never snapped such hot photos, had never had such a fantastic model. Pure and simple, she was a natural—if she didn't land them in jail first.

When she ducked into the changing tent for another suit, giving him a chance to catch his breath, he sank onto the sand. His back rested against a spiny coconut tree, as he stared out to sea. A gigantic cruise ship cut through the waves on its way out of port. The brutal sun sent him reaching for the sunblock.

"Eddie, can you help me in here?" A sweeter voice had never called to him, literally or figuratively.

"Sure thing." He wondered what she needed as he scrambled to his feet. Sauntering over to the tent, he slipped into the dim coolness.

"The strap broke and I thought you might be able to help me fix it." She twisted around, trying without success to reach the slippery strap hanging down her back. Seemingly unabashed, she faced him. One side of her bikini top hung down over her stomach revealing a bare breast.

It wasn't as if it was the first time he'd seen her naked, but damned if she wasn't treating him to a come-hither smile calculated to make him forget work and ravish her inside this tent. "I didn't bring a pin with me. Forget that one and put on the silvery foil one there."

Waltzing up to him, she reached around and unsnapped her bra, letting it puddle on the ground at her feet. Then she lifted his shirt slowly and removed it, letting it sink on top of her bra. Wantonly, she stepped closer, rubbing her breasts across his chest, making the earth quake beneath his feet. "Can I help you put on some more sunscreen?"

Her breasts pressed against his chest felt like heaven and it was all he could do to breathe. Her hands caressed his chest, teasing him unmercifully. He wasn't about to wage war with his mutinying feet to force them to back away from her. Unable to resist her offer, he nodded. "It couldn't hurt."

"Why don't you model?" Hadn't she heard of personal space, or maybe she didn't believe in it as her nipples grazed him all the time she circled him, applying lotion.

When her fingertips drew dangerously near his waistband, he drew in a ragged breath.

"We would make a great team," she said, rubbing her flat palms over his chest, sending his pulse rate rocketing out of control.

Eddie's pulse skittered dangerously and he could feel the vein bulging in his neck. He had no doubt they would make a fantastic team. But he needed time to wrap his mind around her bohemian ways and didn't know if he could match her carefree outlook on life. Not to mention there hadn't been time for his investigation to produce any results. "We hardly know each other…" And yet, even as he spoke, the strange familiarity returned, gnawing at him, making a liar of him. He couldn't decide if she was an angel or a demon, but she was definitely a very dangerous temptress.

* * * * *

Eddie was so hot, his flesh slick and shiny so that all Diana wanted to do was rub against him and drive him as crazy as he was driving her. Reaching out, she tickled him under his chin and licked her lips evocatively. Simmering, she allowed her hungry gaze to devour him as his was consuming her. "You like?"

His shallow respiration told her that he liked the view very much. Overpowering her, his pheromones mixed with her own, making for a very explosive combination.

Her bared nipples puckered and she glanced down at them in amazement. Her cat teats had never reacted this way.

Eddie's gaze was glued on her every movement and he stood rock still, with the notable exception of the growing, fascinating bulge in his suit. One thing that fascinated her more than her own nude human form was his nude body. Male humans were drop-dead gorgeous just like the males of most species. Her own species — correction, her former species — was an exception.

She missed his salty, tangy taste, and longed to run her tongue down his bare chest, seeking previously forbidden territory. No longer would she have to restrict herself to licking his fingers, his face or nibbling his earlobes. It looked as if he would welcome her licking some other very intimate, exciting places. Why humans had to hide their beautiful bodies, she'd never understand. The big yellow ball in the sky certainly warmed their hairless flesh. Clothes were too stifling and uncomfortable, even swimsuits.

Blatantly watching her every move, he stood stoically.

* * * * *

"Do you want to photograph me like this?"

Eddie gulped. "You'd make the loveliest centerfold I've ever seen but, uh, I don't do that type of photography."

Aware that a pout played about her lips, she sidled up to him. "You don't think men would want to see me in only *half* a swimsuit?" Royally irked, she drew on her bikini bottom. Throwing the tent flap open, she marched into the daylight toward a group of young men who were playing volleyball.

Eddie chased after her, kicking up sand behind him. "You can't stroll around Fort Lauderdale Beach almost naked," he hissed. "Get back here."

Tossing her silky mane behind her shoulders, she slapped him in the face with it. "I'm going to prove a point."

Before he could stop her, she waved jovially and called out in her most sugary voice, "Can you big strong men do me a favor?" She struck a sexy pose, jutting her perky breasts out, reveling in her feminine power.

The men turned, their eyes widening, and the volleyball bonked one of them in the head, dazing him. His pack deserted him, and prowled over to her like a herd of tomcats in heat.

"Anything we can do for you," a lanky young man drawled, his ponytail bunched on his sinewy neck.

One of his shorter, stouter buddies elbowed him out of the way, and advanced on her, puffing out his paunchy chest. "Whatever you want, darlin'. You need a man?"

She let herself purr, well aware that Eddie was practically growling behind her like a thwarted mate. Enjoying the male adulation, she turned up the sunniness of her smile and dangled the bikini top off her fingertip. "I need your masculine opinions, gentlemen. Would you buy this bikini for your girlfriends if you saw an ad with me wearing only half the suit?"

"You betcha, darlin'."

"Hell, yeah!"

"I'd buy out the store!"

Scowling deeply, pinpointing her with his dark glare, Eddie draped her with his T- shirt and ushered her back to the tent. "You wanna get gang-banged and wind up in jail?" He added under his breath, "If not worse."

"Gang-banged?" She tried out the unfamiliar term on her lips. "What is that?"

Eddie faced off against her once they were back inside the dim tent, his fists anchored on his hips. "Two seconds more and the whole horde of them were about to jump you in public."

She frowned, mourning her former, excellent night vision. How could humans function so well with such poor eyesight? And they were too stiff to jump well. She missed her former agility. She couldn't even leap onto the kitchen counter without risking serious injury. Frowning, she tried to puzzle out his meaning. "Jump?"

Understanding dawned and she beamed up at him, pleased with herself. "You mean *hump*?"

A strange expression flickered across his eyes and disappeared so quickly she wondered if she'd imagined it. She hated being so blind, so clumsy and almost helpless. Besides losing her sharp sight, she'd also lost her keen sense of smell, so she couldn't pick up his scent to accurately assess his emotional level.

"Strange way to put it, but yeah. We're damned lucky some thief didn't make off with all my camera equipment while you were pulling your little stunt." Seething anger bristled off him.

"You're mad at me."

His nostrils flaring, his eyes quagmires in his shadowy face, he brimmed over with negative energy. "Damn straight."

Trapped. Her hackles rose and the hair on the back of her neck prickled.

Then he released a pent-up sigh and shoveled shaky fingers through his hair. "I'm the boss. I make the decisions and I won't have nude models in my photos, and especially not in the middle of a gang of horny college boys!"

Boss as in master?

Suddenly, the idea of a master didn't appeal to her. She'd been independent as a cat, and she still valued her independence as a human. More and more daily.

Thrusting her chin out, she shrugged out of his shirt and thrust it at him, fire leaping in her veins. "You're making a big mistake, *boss*. Sex sells." Her study of TV had led her to that conclusion. Humans stayed in heat all the time, not merely two or three times a year. They must have a much harder time breeding if they needed such a strong sex drive. Now that she was one of them, her body had burgeoned and was aroused whenever Eddie came near her, whenever she heard his voice, even over the box he called a telephone. Just thinking about the man made her so hot she was about to burn to a crisp.

Perversely, she was hot in more ways than one right now. Almost mad enough to bare her fangs, she fought off the giddy, tingly sensation threatening to overwhelm her.

"Sex isn't everything. Get dressed so we can get out of here before we have more trouble." He clasped her bikini top and then dressed himself and flung his camera over his shoulder.

His reaction stung more than water in her face would have. If this kept up, her mission would fail miserably.

"If the tent's a rockin', don't go knockin', bro'," an unfamiliar and snide voice taunted.

"See what I mean? Rotten punks." Eddie swore under his breath as he took the tent down and tucked it under his arm. He marched away, kicking up sand.

She ran after him, the ocean breeze whipping her long locks away from her face, chilling her. She didn't like it when Eddie was angry.

"Ready for round two with a real man, cutie? I'll make your every dream come true," a foolish young man said, eyeing her brazenly as he ignored Eddie. "I guarantee you; I can do a lot more for you than this old dude."

She eyed the over-inflated oaf disdainfully and turned to Eddie. She didn't like the man's attitude and sensed it was time to make their escape. Clasping his hand in hers, she cajoled, "Let's go home."

Eddie didn't budge except to plant his feet firmly apart in a parade rest position. "Apologize to the lady," he demanded, his eyes narrowed wickedly.

She hissed in a deep breath and stepped between them, not impressed by this misplaced male show of bravado on her behalf, just the opposite. She much preferred the caring, loving man who had cleaned her off and dressed her so tenderly, the one who had worshipped her body. "That's not necessary. Let's go home."

The man laughed and his friends joined in. "She got you whipped, pal?"

"Doesn't sound like much of an apology." Eddie's fists clenched at his side.

Diana grabbed Eddie's arm and tugged. "They're not worth it." She wasn't worth him getting hurt nor did she didn't want any of them to get injured. When tomcats scrapped, they always came out bloody with chunks of their ears missing. Eddie's ears were adorable just the way they were and she didn't want any part of him damaged.

She could feel him seething beneath her fingers and her hopes dwindled for a peaceful resolution. When tomcats caught scent of a female in heat, they didn't back down easily. If she was in heat, it was only for Eddie, but these young men couldn't tell the difference. She felt more than a small measure of guilt for igniting their anger.

Finally, after an interminable amount of time while the sun blazed upon her head, and perspiration trickled between her breasts, Eddie snorted. "The lady's right. You're not worth it."

Pivoting on his heel, spewing burning sand behind him, he strode away so quickly that she was forced to trot to keep up with him. An ominous shadow overtook her and she sucked in a ragged breath, mere seconds before the lanky bruiser grabbed Eddie's shoulder, spun him around and flattened him on the sand.

Her hackles instantly rising, she reverted to attacking feline and she hissed. Baring her fangs, she scratched the attacker's face leaving angry red welts.

The man scrambled away from her on his knees, shooting frightened glances over his shoulder. "Stay away from me, crazy bitch. Or I'll press charges."

Breathing hard, her muscles bunching, she yelled after him, "You attacked first! We'll press charges!"

"Back off, warrior princess," Eddie said, panting, holding her back. "We'd best leave before he returns with his buddies for round two. Help me get the rest of the equipment. It's a wonder it's all still here."

She kept close watch on the man out of the corner of her eye as she hurriedly gathered equipment. She made a note to herself—do not flirt with other tomcats.

* * * * *

When they arrived home, she itched to escape Eddie's foul mood. The beach had been claustrophobic with crowds crushing in on her. A commune with nature had always acted as salve before so why not still? "I'm going for a walk. I haven't gotten any exercise today."

Eddie locked up the sedan and peered at her over the roof, his reflection wavering across the shiny metal. A soft breeze stirred his hair, tossing it over his forehead softening his brooding expression. "Yeah. Sure. I need a cold shower. Be careful of the canal."

Canal…

Horror of horrors.

Tensing, hideous memories crashed over her. Although the sun blazed down on her head, and there wasn't a gray cloud in the sky, she was suddenly cold.

"An alligator almost grabbed one of the neighborhood kids." After a long pause, he stared at the murky waters. "It killed my pet."

She started to nod, and then bit back her agreement. He would think it odd that she knew that bit of information. Instead, she laid a gentle hand on his forearm. "I'm so very sorry to hear that. You must miss her terribly."

He tensed and looked up at that. "Her? You heard about it?"

Rats!

Conversational mousetraps abounded all over the place.

"One of the neighbors mentioned it to me. I saw several pictures of her. She must have been very special for you to photograph her so much."

Shutters slammed down on his expression. "Yep. Look, I'm still raw and don't want to talk about it. That damned gator has never been caught so be careful."

Double rats!

Her breath caught in her throat. The fiend could still be lurking about? Bone-deep fear almost paralyzed her. "Don't worry. I'll stick to the road."

"Good idea." Eddie pulled his arm from her grasp and backed toward the front door. "I hope I didn't scare you too badly. Just be careful and stay clear of the canal."

Too late. Mention of that monster was guaranteed to send her into a tizzy.

Conflicting emotions assaulted her and she hugged herself. But she wasn't alone in her pain. His pain made her ache, and she couldn't tell him that she hadn't really left him. But the love in his voice warmed her heart. So she had been truly special to him. "Okay. I'll be very careful. Promise."

Nodding, Eddie disappeared into the house without another word. When the door slammed behind her and the windows rattled, she winced.

A mama duck with a dozen ducklings waddled past them as they shook water from their feathers. Her mouth watering, her gaze devoured them. She well knew that mother duck. It had escaped her clutches on more than one occasion and attacked her once. Amazed the bird couldn't sense her as the enemy that it passed by leisurely as if she was no threat, her rapt gaze followed it. Well, she wasn't a huntress any longer, was she? Those days were gone forever. Yet the fat bird fascinated her and made her salivate.

She ambled down the quiet road toward the church steeple protruding over a cluster of lofty pine trees. Halfway down the road she spied a chubby yellow tabby cat lazing on a sun-dappled section of grass under a large mimosa tree.

She recognized her good friend Trinity and called out to her softly. The moment the meow left her lips, she gasped and put her hand to her mouth, praying no one had overheard her. Checking out the neighboring yards, she didn't detect any humans nearby.

Trinity squeezed an eye open and peered up at her. She meowed softly, "Do I know you? Your scent reminds me of an old friend."

She crossed the yard, the long blades of grass tickling her ankles, the clover soft and spongy beneath her new beaded sandals. Lowering herself to the grass beside the cat, she tucked her legs to the far side away from her friend. Again she meowed softly, happy she could still understand and speak the language. "It's me. Your friend, Diamond."

"Diamond passed on to the next world." Trinity's brows drew together and her tail stilled. "You are trying to trick me."

Diana tucked her long, messy locks behind her ears and gazed deeply into her friend's eyes. "I speak the absolute truth. How many humans do you know who can speak in the feline tongue? I have been resurrected in this new form. It was my reward for saving the neighbor boy's life."

Trinity didn't blink but she clawed the clump of grass under her paws as she was wont to do when she had something heavy to ponder. Her amber eyes glowed and she hunched back away from Diana. "You could be a demon."

"Remember that time we fought Brutus the bully?" Brutus was the ex-neighbor's vicious Doberman. "I got caught under the fence and when you distracted him until I could wiggle out, he almost killed you?" Memories of that day still haunted her, sending shivers down her spine. It made her very happy his family had moved, even though she now stood taller than the beast.

"I remember." But Trinity still looked at her as if she had three tails and two heads.

"How about the time I confided to you that I was in love with my master and you told me I was crazy?" She picked a three-leaf clover and twirled it in her fingers, sniffing its sweet fragrance and delighting in the summery smells she had always loved so much. Tempted to chew on the scrumptious green clover as she had loved to do, she took a little nibble and licked her lips.

Um, scrumptious!

"Diamond loved clover, too." Awe wove through Trinity's gravelly contralto. "I've never seen a human eat clover before."

"Diamond still does. Is it so hard to believe in reincarnation? Or that I'm Diamond? Mother Earth renews herself every spring. Beings like us are renewed, too."

"No one else has ever come to me before and told me they were reincarnated. Why not if it happens all the time?"

Diana took another bite of the green delicacy, pondering the riddle. "Most beings are reborn as infants with their memories erased. The goddess who resurrected me said she was rewarding me for my sacrifice, that my time on Earth wasn't up yet, that she was allowing me to live out my allotted time as a human because my dearest wish was to become Eddie's human mate. I wished for him to love me as much as I love him."

"Maybe," Trinity drawled, licking her paw. "Sounds like a human thing."

She brought out the heavy artillery. Trinity couldn't overlook this tidbit of knowledge. "Remember how you confided in me that you were going to have Sinbad's kittens?"

Trinity's awed gaze clashed with her. "I didn't confide in anyone but Diamond."

Bingo!

She whispered in her friend's ear, "If I wasn't Diamond, would I know?"

"Diamond, it is you! It's been so long since I've seen you." Trinity licked her outstretched hand with her sandpapery tongue.

Hallelujah! Finally!

"We had four beautiful kittens. All have found homes but one." Trinity ambled to her feet and stretched, her tail rising toward the sun. "Come meet my little darling. I'm afraid my master will take her to the humane shelter if she doesn't find a home soon."

Diana shuddered. *Doomed.* She followed Trinity to the back porch where the kitten roamed about. Like her mother, she was a yellow tiger-striped tabby with soulful topaz eyes. She clapped her hands together in delight and smiled. "She's gorgeous like her mama, who is my very good friend. If she's the last one left, the others must have been stunning."

Trinity joined her kitten, sighed, and treated her to a tongue bath. "She's shy of strangers. Humans all want Mrs. Personality."

Tell her about it. She well remembered.

Diana bent low so as not to frighten the little girl. She winked conspiratorially. "I know a few cat secrets so I bet she'll like me. What do you call her?"

"Rosie because she likes to eat my master's rose petals. She says they taste better than catnip."

"Come here, Rosie," Diana called, holding out her hand and fluttering her fingers. She clucked her tongue as well, the way Eddie used to call her in from a nighttime jaunt outdoors.

Diana meowed softly, imploring the kitten to visit her. "Would you like to come home and live with me? I live down the road so you could still visit your mama."

"You won't get a better home," Trinity said, nudging her little one with her nose. "You couldn't find a more ideal place."

"But I don't want to leave you, Mama." The pathos in Rosie's high-pitched voice broke Diana's heart. Her eyes moist, she rubbed against her mother. "I want to stay with you. I love you."

Trinity kissed her baby. "I love you, too, precious. But our master won't permit you to stay. At least this way you will be close and we can visit. Auntie Diamond will keep her word. She's family."

"I promise," Diana said choking back hot tears, crossing her heart. She remembered how she'd been stolen from her mother, never to see her again. She'd not thought of her in a long time but sudden intense longing assailed her and she vowed not to let that happen to Trinity and Rosie. "We'll visit a lot."

Trinity prodded the kitten again, pushing her forward with her nose. "Go on, darling. Meet your new family."

Rosie ambled slowly, looking over her shoulder at her mother who nodded to her and smiled tremulously.

"You won't find another human who speaks our language, dear. Or another house on the same block." Trinity wiped a tear from her cheek and turned her face away quickly.

So bittersweet. She blinked back tears, trying not to get choked up.

Trinity's human, a large shaggy man with tangled red hair and soda-bottle thick eyeglasses, strolled onto the porch regarding her with undisguised curiosity. "Uh, can I help you?"

Rats! Caught!

Diana jumped to her feet knowing that humans did not take intrusion into their personal space by other people kindly. So new to being a woman, she had forgotten to worry about that until the homeowner had appeared wearing a suspicious look on his ruddy face. "I, uh, found your kitten running around in the road and I was afraid she'd get hit by a car so I was just bringing her back."

The man nodded and stood sentinel-like by the door, his burly arms crossed over his chest. Sun stars glinted off his thick lenses, and she had trouble reading his expression for the glare.

She wanted to work her way around to the subject of adopting Rosie but she couldn't very well tell him that her friend Trinity had been the one to tell her that the kitten was up for adoption. "She's so little and I didn't want her to get hurt. I'm a cat lover from way back." Backing up she winked at Trinity when the man studied Rosie speculatively. "I'm sure you have a lot of things to do. I'll be on my way."

The man's jade eyes lit up in calculation and he stroked his hairy chin. He tilted his unkempt head at the kitten. "You like that kitten there, young lady? She's in need of a good home and I bet she'd love to go home with you. She's the last one left of her litter."

This was almost too easy. Could Venus have set this up?

"I'd love to adopt her!" Diana hoped Eddie wouldn't mind if she brought Rosie home, but he needed a new cat to replace her and Napoleon needed someone to keep him in line. He was getting entirely too comfortable as the sole animal in the house. "Should I take her now?"

"The sooner the better. She's a cute little gal but one cat's my limit. This will be my old Trinity's last litter, yesiree." He bent over and scratched Trinity on her head to soften his words.

"We live just down the road so they'll be able to visit." Diana paved the way for future visits, crossing her fingers that Trinity's owner would be amenable to the idea, as her heart went out to her friend.

"I'm sure Trinity won't mind that a bit. Well, if you'll excuse me, my favorite show is on and I'm missing the babes." He tickled Rosie under her chin. "Have a good life, you lucky girl. You got yourself a pretty lady to love you."

It seemed she was the lucky one. She got to take Rosie home with her. Scooping the kitten into her arms, she nestled her to her heart.

The man turned to go then paused and pivoted on his heel. "Word of warning. Don't let the cat go near the canal. We had a big daddy of a gator 'round these parts recently that got another cat. Bad scene. You'd think the wildlife guys would've caught it by now. We got a lot of kids running around this neighborhood."

Alligator...

No one would let her forget. It seemed to follow her everywhere.

Diana's blood froze in her veins and she shuddered. Most definitely, she would have a good talking to Miss Rosie and explain the facts of Florida life including alligators, cars, dogs, ducks and other hazards. She'd start with the alligator and then how to handle Napoleon. "We'll keep a close eye on her. Nice to meet you."

On the walk home, Diana told the kitten about Eddie. "Eddie's the sweetest, kindest, most loving human you'll ever meet. You'll adore him and be very happy that I brought you home to live with us."

"I hope so." Rosie looked dubious. "Are you sure he'll want me? He's not even met me yet."

Hopefully...

How could anyone not love this adorable little girl?

Eddie really needed a cat to balance out the dog and to replace the void Diamond's absence had left in his life. Trying to convince herself as much as the kitten, Diana pasted a positive smile on her face and nodded. "Of course he will! He loves cats and you're just so adorable; how can he help but fall in love with you at first sight?"

"You'll be there, too, right? You won't leave me alone with him?"

"Of course I'll be there with you!" Diana lifted the tiny creature so that she was eye-level with her, and then realized how she'd started to tremble. Mad at herself, she'd forgotten that the kitten would be scared of such great heights. "You and I are a team from now on. We're family. I'm Auntie Diamond, remember?"

"Promise?"

"Cross my heart." She'd learned that expression from the old movies she'd become addicted to watching. They were such treasure-houses of knowledge, she'd vouch to everyone how wonderful they were.

Diana scratched Rosie under her chin, setting her at ease. She was such a nervous little thing. She'd have to have a good talking-to at Napoleon to be on his best behavior with her, especially while she was still such a baby.

"Huh?" Rosie tilted her head and gave her a blank stare.

"That means, I promise with all my heart." At least she thought that's what it meant. Anyway, that's what she meant when she said it.

The front door loomed in front of them, and Diana paused, staring at it.

Okay, it was now or never…

Mustering her courage, she took Rosie inside, pausing in the entryway to let her eyes adjust to the dim light. "This is your new home, baby," she whispered so no one could hear her but Rosie with the possible exception of the dog.

Rosie's eyes opened wide as she gazed around at her new domain. Scrunching up her nose, she sniffed and recoiled, her fur standing on end. "I smell a dog."

"That's just Napoleon." Diana stroked the cat's furry head, loving the silky feel of it. "He's Eddie's other pet. He's not half bad for a dog. Since he didn't greet us at the front door that must mean that he's in the backyard."

Thankfully.

Napoleon's ebullient greetings would have frightened her new baby for sure. She was much too young to lose one of her nine lives. She'd have to talk to Napoleon about how to behave around the new family member.

"I don't like dogs. They scare me." Tiny sharp claws kneaded Diana's hand.

"Napoleon's a nice dog. You'll like him. He's just like a big, scroungy cat." A big, scroungy, *noisy* cat. She couldn't believe she called him *nice*, or that she truly meant it. Surprisingly, however, she felt good about her assertion. The dog must have mellowed with age.

That or he was just a lot nicer to humans than to cats.

"Eddie? Are you upstairs?" She didn't hear the shower running. The only sound she heard was the whir of the appliances. Either he'd gone out to his office, up to bed, or into the backyard. She headed for the office.

She knocked softly on the door and waited for a reply. One came from the area of his darkroom. "I have something to show you, Eddie. Could you come out here?"

"Just give me a couple secs. I'm almost done developing this roll."

Eager to introduce the new addition to their family to Eddie, Diana rocked back and forth on the balls of her feet, as the seconds ticked away. When he emerged, she held Rosie up. "Eddie, I want you to meet, Rosie, your new kitten. Rosie, I want you to meet Eddie, your new master."

Thunder and dismay warred on Eddie's face making her wish she'd sought his permission even though the chance to keep her friend's kitten in the area had been too good an opportunity to pass up. When their gazes clashed, her heart plummeted to her feet and she cuddled the kitten protectively to her chest.

"Uh oh," Rosie cried, hiding her face against Diana's chest. "He *hates* me."

Oh no! This wasn't going as planned.

But she took comfort in the knowledge that Eddie was too much of a cat lover to hate Rosie, but she couldn't voice the assurance with him standing within earshot.

"Don't you think I should have been consulted before you decided to adopt an animal and bring it into my house?" He eyed Rosie warily, reviving her skittishness, not at all what Diana wished to happen.

Ouch!

Quelling the frisson of alarm running up her arms, Diana raised her chin, refusing to back down. "I thought it'd do you good to adopt a new cat." She held out the sweet kitten to him, but he remained remote.

"If I wanted another pet, I'd choose one."

If left to his own devices, he might never adopt another cat. She couldn't take Rosie back. What would happen to her? Alarmed by Eddie's hardened, stubborn heart, she stroked the little darling behind her ears and crooned to her. "But she needs you and you need her. Cats are good for you. Please."

Eddie shook his head. "I had my last cat for three years. Give a guy a chance to grieve."

But Rosie needed a home now...

Diana lowered herself by him and perched on the end of the couch. "You can still grieve for your old pet but I'm sure she'd want you to be happy and give a good home to this sweet little thing."

Eddie stared at Rosie for several excruciating moments before his countenance softened a tad. "I guess she's sort of cute."

Rosie frowned up at her and meowed, "He's still not sure he wants me here. Where will I go? What will I do?"

Since she couldn't answer verbally around Eddie, she hugged her all the while wanting to thump some sense into the stubborn man.

Eddie reached over to pet her and Rosie swiped his hand with her sharp claws. When a string of curses tripped off Eddie's lips in harmony with Rosie's screams, Diana's heart skipped several beats.

Oh no!

With a terrified expression, the kitten leapt out of her arms and dashed across the room. Hiding under the couch in one of Diamond's favorite hiding places, the only thing visible was her glowing eyes.

Eddie's scowl returned and he was rubbing his hand, hissing in a shallow breath. "The little vampire drew blood." Red-stained fingers lowered to his lap. "Has she had her shots yet?"

"Shhh. Stop yelling. You'll scare Rosie." Diana closed the distance between them, took his hand in hers, and examined his wound.

"Rosie, huh? Not Vampirella?" Sarcasm oozed from his lips. "What do you mean I'll scare her? The little bloodsucker scares me."

"Rosie," she said firmly as she climbed onto the couch and kneeled so she could get close enough to help. The little scoundrel had dug a couple claws fairly deep, drawing blood. "And stop calling her names. She's a sweet little baby."

"About as sweet as a baby tarantula."

Had Eddie always been so insufferable? Funny how she'd never noticed it in her former life…

Diana rolled her eyes. "You'll live. Let me doctor it up for you." She had the insane desire to lick his wound but that would be a dead giveaway. Within moments she was cleansing and bandaging the wound under his direction.

A ghost shimmered behind Eddie, floating in the air. Venus' image materialized and she put her finger to her lips and then pointed to the next room in unmistakable command.

She groaned. *Not now.*

Swallowing her dismay, hoping Eddie didn't notice her discomfiture, she tried to mask her surprise. "Excuse me a moment. I left something in the other room." Before Eddie could question her, she made her escape, trying not to run and raise his suspicions.

Venus hovered high in the kitchen, her arms folded across her chest, her lips pursed. Her expression grim, she shook her head. "I'm disappointed. You let me down."

Diana's heart plummeted to her feet and she veiled her eyes with her lashes. Digging her nails into her palms, she tried to stay her quivering nerves. "I'm sorry things got out of control. It's not easy being human."

"My father wants me to change you back into a feline. He thinks the episode at the beach proves you can't overcome your basic nature."

No! This couldn't be happening. Her time couldn't be up yet.

Bending on her knees, she clasped her hands and gazed imploringly up at the ethereal being. "Oh please, your grace, grant me another chance. I'm learning. It's so much more wonderful and scary than I ever dreamed. I'm trying so very hard."

"If I do, I'll be sticking out my neck for you. Father has not been happy with me for the past thousand years. He believes me out of control and has a motion into the council to place me under restriction."

Sad that she had brought trouble upon her patron, Diana hung her head and scuffled her feet on the smooth tile. "I would never deliberately be a nuisance or cause you humiliation. If you give me another chance, I promise I will remember my place and act accordingly. Please, please let me remain a woman. Let me stay with Eddie."

The etched line of the goddess' lips softened and she sighed. "You are a sweet, well-meaning creature; therefore, I will grant you another chance. But don't forget, you are being watched."

Thank heaven!

Diana closed her eyes in relief. "Thank you. You won't regret believing in me. I'll make you proud."

"Just make yourself proud, little one. Be happy." Venus blew her a kiss and disappeared.

"Who are you talking to?" Eddie strolled into the kitchen a split second after the goddess evaporated, making her heart race.

What a close call!

Diana forced herself to breathe and smile. "I just called the doctor. He said not to worry, just to bandage you up as I was doing."

Eddie nodded, accepting her explanation. "I want to talk to you about our next shoot. Let's conference at the table."

Chapter Six

Diana was awakened by the click of the door and whispery footsteps on the carpet. She squeezed the sleep from her eyes and rolled toward the muffled sound.

What delicious smells!

She sniffed appreciatively.

Eddie's unmistakable scent—a little musky and pure ambrosia—mingled with the unmistakable smell of meat. Peering into the night, she made out his outline as he stealthily approached her in the moonlight. Tall. Powerful. Mysterious. Utterly beautiful.

Ice tinkling in the glass he held out, he stared down at her before speaking in muted tones, "How are you feeling? I brought you a peace offering for being such a bear earlier."

His voice couldn't sound more beautiful if he had just professed undying love and devotion. Well maybe, but not much. Yawning, she stretched languidly. The thin material of her nightgown strained against her tingling chest. Still half-asleep, her thoughts tumbled out unguarded. "You know you have the richest, sexiest voice I've ever heard?" Not that she had all that much experience with human males, but she'd been watching a lot of television, especially the cooking and educational channels, since her transformation and Eddie could go up against sexy rock stars any day. She'd also grown quite fond of several afternoon soap operas which were teaching her a lot about true human love.

He thrust a food bag and a glass of ice water toward her. Propping herself up on her elbow, she favored him with her prettiest smile. Food would be a super highway to her heart if he didn't already own it. Not long ago she'd have followed a man anywhere for the scent of raw beef.

Gratefully, she took the glass from him and let the cool liquid slide down her throat. Gazing up at him dreamily, she nibbled on the gourmet dinner spread out on the nightstand. This was almost as divine as Heaven.

Sparking fire, Eddie's eyes darkened. A myriad of thrilling emotions flickered across his chiseled features, fascinating her. "You look like an angel bathed in silvery moonlight." Then he backed away a step. "I shouldn't have said that. It just slipped out."

Oh yes he should have. He could compliment her all he wanted. The more, the better.

Desire coiling in her stomach, joy flooded her. "And you look like a devil." She couldn't defy the mischief dancing in her soul, and curled sensually upon the bed, knowingly seducing her boss.

When passion clouded his eyes, she licked her suddenly parched lips. Only his wet tongue could restore their moisture and she longed for a rainstorm. Maybe even a hurricane.

"Diana." His raspy voice excited her, but it was his rapidly swelling cock that stole her breath and coaxed hot juices to flow between her legs. She squirmed against the smooth, sweat-slick sheets.

He was so incredibly hot!

"Eddie." She held her hand out to him, inviting him into her bed. This night he would know who he was making love to, no delusions or pretenses. Except for the grandmother of deceptions—that she was once his sweet cat.

Though his respiration increased, he hesitated. He couldn't fool her. She could smell his desire. He lusted after her.

Maybe he didn't know how much she longed for him, how deeply she craved to be held in his arms, to be in his life. Nearly on fire, she scooped an ice cube out of her drink, slid it over her burning chest, and let it slip through her fingers down her cleavage. "I'm so hot."

"I could turn down the air conditioning." His ragged voice broke huskily as his rapt gaze devoured her.

Like that could quell the fire raging in her?

She shook her head and grasped the bottom of her gown and lifted it a tantalizing inch at a time until she revealed her navel. "Or I could just remove these annoying clothes." Without waiting for his answer, she lifted the gown and tugged it off. She remained kneeling, her chest thrust out.

Eddie gulped, his eyes deep pools of desire. His slacks strained across his hips with the force of his erection. His gaze starved, he walked toward her slowly, inexorably. "So ravishing."

Bewitched by his ravenous expression, power surging through her, she pushed out her taut nipples to him. He cupped a full breast in his hand, testing its weight. Then he bent his head and tasted it, suckling gently. Moaning, he nibbled it then pulled it hard into his eager mouth.

Such exquisite sensations.

She arched against him, rubbing against him, longing to feel his bare flesh against her nipples. She unbuttoned his shirt and spread her hands beneath it, holding her palm over his erratically beating heart. His scent intoxicated her and she writhed against him.

"How can you be so pure yet so primal?" His breath tickled her and she laughed.

If he only knew…

A purr rumbled deep in her chest, flamed by the lick of his tongue. Felines were pure, noble, and sensual creatures. Even though she had changed in many ways, her basic essence remained the same. How she wished she could tell him the entire truth but dared not. The truth would probably frighten him away. Had she been the human first, would she have believed him if he'd told her that he'd been turned into a cat? Probably not.

Rather than answer vocally, she gave into her basest desire, letting her tongue express her feelings, kissing her way across his face to his ear. She swirled the tip around his earlobe, until he moaned.

Plundering her lips again in a searing kiss, his tongue danced, mating with hers as he drank more deeply of her than she'd ever dreamed possible. He flung her back upon the bed, his weight delightfully heavy upon her. Their hearts pounded together in concert.

A virtual lioness, she tore at his clothes, her fingers fumbling first with the button and then with the zipper of his slacks, hungry to feel his cock pulse wildly in her hands. She had never wanted anything more in her life than to mingle her soul, her life with his.

Greedy to have all of him, she pushed his pants off his hips and wrapped her fingers around his satiny, engorged cock. Awed by the blood pounding through it, at how it could be so hard and hot, yet so smooth and silky at the same time, she stroked it tenderly. Parting the slit on the end, she smiled when his seed oozed out.

Her own lubrication flowed readily and she parted her legs wide so that he fit more snugly between her thighs, so that their coarse curls tangled as their hips ground together in the ancient dance of love.

Wanting to prolong the pleasure and glory, she wriggled out from beneath him, escaping his strong embrace. When he began to protest, she licked her way down his hard, muscled length, tasting his salty muskiness.

How very tasty he was.

She enjoyed drawing out his pleasure, teasing and tempting him. She pushed his restrictive clothing off then swirled her tongue across the flat, hard planes of his abs. Working her way down his length, she followed the trail of hair that started at his belly button leading straight to his cock. Intoxicated by his scent, she licked around the base of his cock as it flexed and throbbed, careful not to touch it with her tongue but rubbing her cheeks against the raging inferno.

"Temptress," he accused on a ragged breath as she nibbled her way down the inside of his legs, her hair grazing his balls.

Smiling against his powerful legs, she licked her way down to his feet and treated them to a tongue bath, one toe at a time. How wonderful it would feel when those legs wrapped around her, imprisoning her against him as he plunged his cock into her core. Biting her lower lip as hard as she could to stop the trembling sensation, she nearly came at the thought. How she wanted to pleasure him all over. She worked her way back up the front of his foot as she massaged the other one between her hands. Reveling in his flavor, she loved how he flexed and writhed beneath her, how his growl rumbled deep in his stomach and coursed all the way down through his extremities.

"You like this." It wasn't a question. She barely recognized the husky voice emanating from the depths of her soul as her own.

"Um...don't stop."

Feeling decidedly wicked, she nipped his calf and continued her journey up his inner thigh to the jewels she sought. "If I don't stop that, I can't do this." She positioned her head between his legs. Propping herself up on her elbow, she gazed upon his incredible erection. "So beautiful."

More than beautiful.

"Ditto." He ran a finger along her velvety folds, then probed her gently. When he rubbed her clit, she moaned.

Not to be outdone, she traced the bulging vein that thrummed up his cock with the tip of her fingernail, and then replaced it with her tongue. His writhing excited her so she lapped faster, working her way to the inviting tip. Wanting better access, she rolled on top of him and took his cock into her mouth, sucking hard. Growling, he thrust deeply into her.

Awed at their mass, she cupped his balls reverently with one hand. With her other, she stroked the base of his cock.

He was so magnificent.

Teetering on the periphery of ecstasy, she bucked against his magical hand, her muscles tightening around the two fingers plunging into her mercilessly. Molten lava erupted in her core, flowing over his hand. Wanting to share the glorious explosion with him, she pumped harder and sucked greedily around her pleasurable moans.

"Harder, babe!" Eddie thrust one final time into her mouth. His release was forceful, spewing seed down her throat that spilled down her chin and pooled between her breasts.

How virile!

She drank greedily of him, delighting in his nectar. When he no longer thrust into her mouth, she slid her lips off slowly, excruciatingly so, and then kissed the tip lovingly. "I could drink of you all day."

Eddie gazed upon her lovingly, a passionate gleam in his eyes. He grazed her cheek with his knuckles. "You would be so greedy?"

More than greedy. Absolutely ravenous.

She tilted her head as she stared at his magnificent slick cock only inches from her face. The pulsing shaft wavered in and out of focus the longer she stared at it. "Greedy? Me?"

He scooted around on the bed, crawling between her legs, placing them over his shoulders. "I'm thirsty, too. You wouldn't deny a thirsty man a drink of you, would you?"

Not if that man was Eddie. Only Eddie.

"Definitely not." Her words came out more as a moan for he buried his face between her legs, his lips firmly clamped around her labia, his wicked tongue lapping her juices, wreaking havoc inside her womb.

He was a wizard of love, this one.

She gazed upon his dark head lovingly and shoveled her fingers through his silky locks, massaging his scalp. Wave upon wave of rapture washed over her, threatening to burst her veins, stealing her breath. He ran his fingertip lightly over her, and then worked it slowly into her anus. It was so very scrumptiously, wickedly tight that she bucked against him, pushing her pussy against his face.

Whirling and swirling, stormy desire raged inside her. Lost in the rough seas of emotion, she ground her hips harder against his. Moans and groans rumbled in her chest.

Just as the dam broke, he pulled her high into his arms and shoved his tongue deeper into her, sucking her until he drained every last drop of her juices. Shuddering in his arms, she gulped in air as he lowered her to the mattress.

He crawled up her length, pressing her into the bed. His lips glistened with her womanly juices. He throbbed against her, toying with her, flaming her desire back to life. His cock rubbed against her curls, sliding against her slick vaginal lips in no hurry to gain entry but rather taunting and stoking her fire.

He held himself over her so that his chest grazed her nipples, bringing them to hardened twin peaks. "Demon," she mumbled through her parched lips as she arched upward, eager to mold her breasts to his hard chest.

"How bad do you want it?" He captured her lower lip in his teeth, sucking it into his mouth. His laughter husky, he rubbed his nose against hers.

Desperately!

She didn't have to ask to what he referred. "Oh, yeah. All of it. Deep." Her voice came out in raspy bursts, dissipating into the darkness. With unmistakable invitation, she ground her hips against his, and then slipped her hand between their bodies, seeking the source of his primal heat. Her fingers curled around his thickness, instantly set aflame.

"Oh, yeah." She moaned into his mouth as he crushed her lips beneath his. Simultaneously he thrust his full length into her, their souls intertwining.

He growled against her, exciting her with his primitive reaction. Her tight channel gloved his thickness, absorbing every inch of him as he stroked into her.

She raked her fingernails down his back as she bathed his chest with her tongue. It flicked over his male nipples and around the hard contours of his magnificent chest. All the hours he worked out had really paid off. His physical form was magnificent.

"Um, you taste marvelous," Eddie said.

That made two of them.

Smiling, he lowered a soft kiss to her forehead. "How is it that an enchantress like you hasn't been snagged yet? Maybe you're a control freak?"

Control freak? Hardly…

Closing her eyes against the silvery moonlight dappling the bed, her long lashes tickled her cheeks. Delighting in his perfection, she gazed at him covertly. "My mission is to please you. And how do you know I haven't been snapped up?"

He chuckled, his deep voice a rumble against her chest and he held her hand up to view it. "Don't think I haven't checked out your ring finger. There's not as much as a tan line."

"I've only ever been in love…"

Yikes!

She bit her tongue. Hard.

Horror of horrors, she'd almost confessed that she'd only ever been in love with one man. *Him.* Quickly recovering, she chastised herself for her stumble. "I've only ever been in love…once, a long time ago." The lie fell harshly from her lips. True she had only been in love once in her lifetime, but she had never fallen out of love. Her heart and soul belonged to him. She would give her life for him.

"You can remember? You're not in love now?" Each word was punctuated by a hard thrust into her.

Very much so.

She kissed his nipple, his heart pounding fiercely against her ear. "Yes. I love you."

His rhythm slowed for a moment as he gazed deeply into her eyes. Murky, his gaze smoldered with desire. "This is so fast."

It had been forever…

"How long does it take to fall in love? When it's the real thing?" Of course she couldn't explain how they'd known one another for years. Or that her heart had his name emblazoned on it.

"But this is only our second time." He stroked damp tendrils of hair away from her face gently, his touch mesmerizing.

"Once can be enough." She decided to confess. "But actually, this is our third time. There was another night I came to you…"

He stopped his thrust midway, his hips hard against hers. "That was real? I wasn't dreaming?"

Cross her heart…

"It was real."

"It was wonderful. You were fantastic."

"Was?" She quirked a brow at him and writhed beneath him. She molded her hands to his buttocks and gave him a gentle push.

"You are wonderful." His words were more of a growl.

"You wouldn't leave a lady on the brink of rapture, would you?" She affected a pretty pout as she ground her hips to his trying to appease the ache thrumming deep inside. He was so immense, so long and so hot, fireworks imploded in her womb. She screamed, clutching his arms, digging her nails into his muscularity.

A wicked smile curved his cheeks as he pumped hard into her. Finally, he slammed into her, his body rigid, rocking the bed, shooting his seed deep into her. Shuddering against her, he held her tightly, their hearts beating in unison.

Her lungs aching from the workout, she turned her face away from his chest and gasped for sweet air tinged with their musky odor. His cock still inside her, it flexed, deliciously.

Breathing hard, he slid out of her inch by excruciating inch. Bemoaning the loss of his warmth and possession, she rolled on her side and snuggled against him.

Some time later, he rose on his knees, positioning himself behind her.

"You enjoyed being fucked from behind, didn't you?" He rubbed the velvety tip of his cock across her buttocks. It was so warm, so juicy and satiny, that she trembled against it, sighing.

It seemed so natural.

"Oh, yes." Her admission whooshed out on a contented sigh. She would no more deny her desire for him than to stop breathing. Marveling at his power, she thrilled to feel his strength slamming into her.

He bathed her ear with his tongue, a pleasure she'd not thrilled to since she'd become human. His cock grazed the small of her back then traced a fiery path down the length of her spinal column. He whispered huskily in her ear, "Do you want me to take you from behind now?"

"Oh, yes! Fly us to the moon." She'd longed to say that since watching several old romantic movies on cable. She pressed back against him, digging her elbows into the mattress to boost her from the bed. Then she rolled to her knees and wiggled her butt under his face.

"Ooh, baby, hang on tight. I'll fly you to the heavens." He rolled her nipple between his thumb and forefinger, and then straightened tall, towering over her.

Her tingling breasts swung freely, the sensitized nipples grazing the rumpled sheets as he ran the tip of his cock down the crack of her behind. Her hair curtained her face, swishing around her face as she swayed gently.

What seemed like an eternity later, but in truth was mere moments, he guided his cock between her cheeks, seeking her center. When he was about halfway in, he thrust hard, holding her hips firmly as he pounded into her.

Wildfire consumed her making her drag in precious air, her breathing ragged. Waves of ecstasy crashed through her, carrying her off to an exulted plane of pleasure. Psychedelic colors swirled before her eyes and she moaned aloud.

Her release triggered Eddie's. He thrust into her one final time, clamping her buttocks to his groin, his large hands firm and commanding.

Oh God, it was so wonderful!

They fell together to the bed, his arms snaking around her waist, pulling her back against his chest. His rapidly beating heart pounded against hers and her heart matched his rhythm. Tickling and massaging her, his lips caressed the back of her neck. "I could get used to this."

It wasn't exactly a declaration of undying love, but she'd take what she could get. Embers raged into forest fires. Sparks ignited an inferno. What they'd just experienced constituted far more than mere embers and sparks. With this victory, she was confident that she would win his heart and soul well before her deadline.

Twisting around in his arms, she pressed her naked body to his and looped her arms around his neck. They fit perfectly and she purred her satisfaction. She laid her ear against his steady heartbeat and snuggled closer. "So could I."

Chapter Seven

Eddie couldn't wait to see Diana's expression when he pulled up at their surprise shoot location. She'd look fab swimming with the dolphins making for a dynamite photo for the sports magazine that had hired him to do their annual swimsuit layout. He couldn't wait to see the beautiful model with the magnificent dolphins.

What a dynamite shoot this would be!

Sunlight bathed Diana's silvery locks, the same ones that wound around him nightly. Sunbeams danced across the windshield and steam arose from the baking asphalt. Normally balmy in the mid-nineties with a brisk ocean breeze to cool the peninsula, the water seemed particularly still and calm today. Without the slightest wind to temper the harsh sun, temperatures crept into the low hundreds. Even with the air conditioning on full blast in the van, perspiration ran down Eddie's back. He swiped his hand across his lip to remove the annoying moisture.

"Are we almost there?" Diana asked, unusually edgy.

Was something eating at her?

Something seemed amiss but he couldn't pinpoint it. He wanted her to be relaxed today, not edgy. He needed his beautiful model at her best. A lot of money rode on this shoot.

He forced a smile to his face as his glance slid over at her. "We still have a good half hour to go." He hoped, wondering if his map was accurate. Not that one could get very lost in the Keys. They were one long strip of linked skinny islands sporting one main highway. In places, there was barely enough land to host the two-lane highway. The seaquarium should be large enough that signs would be posted on the thoroughfare to point the way. Surely he could find his destination in broad daylight.

Diana laid a slim hand on his forearm instantly igniting his desire. To her credit, she merely had to gaze at him with those amber eyes to rev his motor. "Where are we going?" Her playful million-dollar pout lingered in her question.

He couldn't wait for her to find out so he had to bite his tongue. She was going to love it.

"A surprise isn't a surprise if I tell you." Whistling happily, he imagined the great photos he would get of her with the graceful sea creatures.

"Why all the mystery?" Diana's eyes grew wide as she gazed at the ocean on either side, so still and silent it could be glass. Her fingers kneaded her legs, a nervous habit he had noted on more than one occasion.

Why was she so tense?

"No mystery. Just fun mixed with a little work." Diana would look awesome riding a dolphin. He was sure this issue of the magazine would be a sellout. And he itched for his turn to swim with the dolphins after the shoot was finished.

He muttered under his breath when an inconsiderate driver pulled out in front of him with no warning and he had to slam on the brakes, causing Diana to jerk forward until the seat belt caught her and bounced her back against the seat.

"You okay?" When she nodded and smiled up at him, he asked, "Is this your first time to visit the Keys?" He tried to sound nonchalant, using supreme effort to keep his gaze on the line of vehicles ahead of him when all he wanted to do was gaze upon her ethereal beauty.

That's all they needed was for him to crash into another vehicle.

Her jittery gaze swiveled around to meet his. "First time. So much water." Trepidation colored her voice, sending a feeling of unease through him again.

"Yep. Water, beach, and sunshine. Florida's vacation playground." A snorkeler, he loved the water. The reef was a photographer's wet dream.

"Sunshine's good." She yawned and stretched, rolling her bare shoulders languidly. Her hardening nipples stood out against the thin material of her dress so he could distinguish the dusky areolas, much to his growing discomfort. The straps of her daffodil-yellow sundress insisted on falling down and only a thin strip of elastic kept the frock in place across her braless chest. If she inhaled too deeply the dress was liable to fall to her waist.

Down boy.

Trapped painfully inside his jeans, his cock stood at attention. His maneuverings proved futile behind the steering wheel. He forced his mind to safer thoughts like icy cold water and the monster car crashes he'd cause if he didn't keep himself under control.

Finally at the billboard advertising the seaquarium he breathed a sigh of relief as he turned in and parked. "We're here."

Diana turned in her seat and tugged on her errant strap. "What is this place?"

"The seaquarium." At her blank stare, he explained, "They keep fish and sea mammals like dolphins and whales."

An almost hungry gleam flickered across Diana's eyes. "I like fish. Do they have tuna salad?"

Eddie blinked. Diana came up with some off-the-wall things, but she was purely refreshing. "Hungry, are we? We'll stop at this little seafood restaurant down the road after we're through with the shoot. We'll lose the light if we don't take the photographs now."

But he couldn't let his model starve. He'd better feed her so she could get her mind back on work. It never failed to amaze him how slim and trim she stayed despite her ravenous appetite.

Digging around in the cooler he brought on long trips, he asked, "Do you want the ham or salami?"

She turned to study the building, her puckered forehead and drooping lips mirrored in the passenger side window. "This isn't a restaurant? We don't get to dine on fish?"

He shook his head and squinted into the brilliantly shining sun. "Afraid not."

"I'll take the ham." She held out her hand and accepted the wrapped food, with a less-than-excited expression.

He got out and jogged around to her side of the van. "No. It's a giant fish bowl. Like a zoo for sea creatures."

"Oh." She took a bite of the sandwich and chewed slowly. Disappointment tinged her voice but her lashes made endearing crescents on her cheeks so that he couldn't glimpse her eyes to judge her thoughts.

He hauled his photography equipment out of the van. "You're going to swim with the dolphins. Trust me, you'll look spectacular next to one of the beauties. It'll sell thousands of magazines. Your picture might even make the cover."

"Isn't it risky?" Diana hung back when they started walking toward the locker rooms.

He stopped and turned back, perplexed by her hesitancy and wide, frightened eyes. He held out his hand to her, coaxing her to relax and join him.

Blood draining from her face, she wavered.

Worried, he retraced his steps to her side and lowered his hand to her shoulder. "Something wrong?"

She hung her head fractionally, silky blonde tendrils falling across her face. Her slight weight shifted from one foot to the other. "I don't know how to swim. I don't like water. And those are Mastiff-sized fish."

Speechless, he gawked at her. He'd never dreamed she couldn't swim. It had never occurred to him to ask her, not after he'd found her strolling alongside the canal. She lived in South

Florida, land of fun in the sun and surf. Who lived here and didn't like water?

"Maybe I can stand beside the water without getting in?"

He'd wanted to share the spiritual experience of swimming with the magnificent creatures with her, and it would have made a dynamite photo spread, but he pushed away the disappointment welling up in his chest. Capturing her hand, he squeezed her fingers, focusing on her needs and comfort. "I'll figure out a different way to do the shoot so you don't have to get in the water."

Every muscle in her tensed up. Only the pulse in her throat hammered away. "Thank you."

He could kick himself for bringing her here, for not finding out this crucial detail about the woman who could make or break his product. No wonder she'd stared out the window like a zombie on the drive down the coast.

So much for surprises. He was the one who had ended up surprised. Maybe he could cut and paste a few pictures together. Graphics programs could work wonders. Now if he could get at least one of the dolphins to jump high in the air for the camera, he could get an awesome shot.

A slender russet-curled pixie wearing the seaquarium uniform, walked briskly toward them, her feet squelching in sodden tennis shoes. Wet footmarks trailed behind her on the concrete deck. "I'm Caitlin and I've been assigned to help you. What do you need to get started?"

"Would it be possible for her to throw fish to the dolphins? Or is there a way to get them to jump out of the water?" Trying to be more attentive to Diana's needs and sensitive to her feelings, he turned to her. "Would you have any objections to touching a fish or throwing it into the water?"

Diana's sunny smile rewarded him. "I like fish. I don't mind touching them."

He tried not to show his surprise. He'd expected her to be more squeamish even though he was happy she wasn't. Most of the women he knew wouldn't touch a whole fish, dead or alive. Eddie squeezed Diana's hands in his and ran the pad of his thumb over the pulse hammering away in her wrist. "You're amazing."

Diana sidled up to him and placed a kiss on his chin. "Not half as amazing as you."

The way Diana gazed up at him turned up his temperature. His cock flexed so that he turned to hide himself from the women's view. He was getting too good at this maneuver.

When Caitlin returned with a burly blond lifeguard who helped her carry buckets of fish, an idea dawned on Eddie. The handsome young man possessed a Herculean physique. "Would you like to earn some extra cash?"

"Sure, dude. Depending on what it is you want me to do." An intrigued expression crossed over his tanned features as his gaze raked over Eddie's camera equipment.

"What's your name?" At thirty-two Eddie felt decrepit compared to this young stud.

"Cliff." The macho name fit the blond surfer.

"Diana, my model, is going to feed the dolphins. But she can't swim, so I thought I'd make it look like she was with graphics. Think you'd like to swim with the dolphins so that I can take pictures of them in the right position? Then I'll paste her in with you later."

"Sounds cool. What kind of money are you talking? Every bit helps pay my college tuition."

Eddie pulled him off to the side and quoted a rate that made the younger man's eyes light up.

"Can't keep Flipper waiting," Eddie said as he ambled back to the women.

"Flipper?" Diana laced her hands behind her and shifted her weight back and forth on her heels. "You know the dolphins already? You've been here before?"

Eddie opened his mouth to explain and then thought better of it. He supposed not everyone watched moldy reruns. Still, didn't everyone over twenty know of the famous dolphin?

Eddie set up his equipment while Cliff gave Diana a tour of the institute. His curious gaze kept sliding to the pair who had their heads bent close together. Every time Diana laughed at something the other man said, he growled. *Great idea. Just hand her to the other guy.*

Although it only took a few minutes to set up the shot, it seemed like hours. He focused the camera lenses and adjusted the lighting.

"Slick back your hair." Eddie ground his teeth at the scene before him. The suit hugged Diana's luscious curves as she leaned intimately against Cliff. Water droplets cascaded down their faces, their chests, and slid into Diana's lucky bra. Eddie's tongue ached to trace their path to Diana's delectable breasts. He could hardly keep his mind on work.

"Diana, throw some fish to the dolphin."

Caitlin stood nearby, just out of camera shot, in case Diana needed help. She offered helpful advice.

When a dolphin came close enough to Diana's hand to kiss her fingers, she jerked back and almost slipped.

"Whoa! Don't break your neck. Just toss the fish to her instead of holding it."

Diana dipped her hand into the bucket and drew out a few fish and held the excess in her left hand as she tossed one at a time to the dolphin with her right.

Amazing. Not many women would do that. Diana was certainly a find. One in a million.

Cliff frolicked with her on deck for a couple rolls worth of film and helped her feed the fish.

"Now, Cliff, act like you're holding Diana. Just play around. Have fun, and I'll do the rest." He'd cut and paste Diana in later.

Before he knew it, he'd shot several rolls of film and caught some fantastic poses. He had to admit they worked well together.

"That's a wrap. Good work." He wrote out a check to Cliff as the young buck climbed out of the pool. Slapping the man on the back, he said, "Good job. Think you'd like to help us out again sometime?"

"Sure thing. Let me give you my phone number." He scribbled his contact information on a piece of scrap paper and handed it to Eddie.

"Nice working with you," Eddie said dryly. Surely, the golden couple would inspire mega sales.

Cliff tossed a lopsided smile his way. "It's been a pleasure, dude. I look forward to working with you again soon."

"I'll set up some more shoots and give you a call. First, let me develop and submit these photos to the magazine. Be on the lookout for some copies."

Diana sidled up to him as he was talking and linked her fingers through his, sparking electricity and reminding him of her promise for later that night. Her stomach growled and he felt a little selfish.

In his eagerness to get the shoot while he had optimum light, he had forgotten that all she'd had to eat this afternoon was a snack. He got too caught up in his work to the exclusion of personal comforts, like eating. He reached deep into his pocket and handed her some cash. "Get yourself something to eat while I pack up. I'd like to swim a little with Flipper, myself. Let me know when you're finished eating and we can stop at a seafood restaurant for a nice dinner on the way home." He gave her a quick kiss and turned his attention to his equipment.

He locked his cameras securely in the back of the van. Not wanting to tempt a thief, he tossed a cover over them. Then he headed to the locker room and changed into his swim trunks. Now Eddie's cock swelled and he held the towel as casually over himself as he could manage and still walk confidently to the pool for a short swim.

Whoa! Who'd dumped ice in the water?

Wasn't this supposed to be the subtropics? His teeth chattering, he rubbed his arms vigorously to create a warming friction.

He swam around solo for a bit to let the dolphins get used to him. Just when he was about to give up and get out, he was pushed from behind and shoved face-first into the water.

He swallowed half a gallon of ocean water and came up spluttering. "What the he—?"

Inhuman laughter taunted him from behind and he whirled around to glare at his tormentor. A huge dolphin rose halfway out of the water and slapped its fins together, laughing.

"Zelda likes you. She's inviting you to play," Caitlin said, trying to suppress a giggle. "Hold your hand out to her and see if she'll come up to you."

Who was she kidding?

"So she can finish drowning me?" He wasn't sure he trusted the mischievous dolphin. And as far as the hand thing went, was she supposed to come up and sniff it or lick it like a dog? Did fish have tongues?

Treading water, he watched Zelda with his peripheral vision. Gentle waves lapped at him, seagulls cawed to each other as they glided overhead, and the sound of distant vehicles hummed softly in the background. This should be an ideal day, so why was he staring down a rabid dolphin while his woman dined alone? Or worse, with the beefcake.

"Come on. Swim closer. She won't hurt you." The pushy lifeguard cheered him on. She leaned back and washed the hair out of her eyes. Then she leaned her head to the side and shook the water from her ears.

Zelda dove into the water causing a monstrous splash. Then Eddie was upended when the huge smooth body swam between his legs. Knocked off balance, he was sucked under into a sea of bubbles and movement. The dolphin nudged his chest with her nose and swished her tail.

Sure, Zelda wouldn't hurt him. Drowning didn't hurt, right?

Holding his breath, he propelled himself upward toward the sunlight streaming down into the murky depths. He surfaced again, his wet hair plastered against his forehead, making it impossible to see. He pushed the sodden mess from in front of his eyes and scowled at the destroyer. "Okay. Okay! I get the message you want to play. So what do I do?"

"Hold onto her and she'll take you for a swim." The young brunette's amused smile encompassed them.

Tentatively, he stroked the smooth gray flesh. Zelda nodded as if giving him permission to touch her or perhaps telling him to hurry up and get off his lazy butt. She squealed at him and sprayed water out the spout on the top of her head, showering him.

"Down girl. I already have a girlfriend." He had to smile at his own joke, but he wondered what was keeping Diana so long. He yearned to taste her sun-kissed flesh.

He grabbed onto Zelda and she sped off, towing him. Before long, Eddie lost himself in the pleasure of swimming with the dolphin, enjoying the salt spray in his face and the hot sun warming his back. A playful creature, she was full of devilment and she was as likely to dunk him as hoist him in the air. She was gentle despite her great strength.

A human finger tapped him on the shoulder, awaking him from his aquatic dream. Whirling around, he was caught off guard by Zelda's sudden turn and knocked into the young lifeguard.

"There's been a problem. Please come with me." Caitlin's formerly friendly voice had cooled several degrees and an arctic chill had iced over her eyes.

"A problem?" Dread washed over him. What kind of problem could there be? Maybe Cliff wasn't permitted to model while on duty. Great! A whole day of shooting wasted. He'd have to destroy the film and start all over.

Pushing his unruly hair out of his eyes, he squinted at the lifeguard as he followed her. He spied Diana on the observation deck, flanked by another brawny lifeguard, a suited executive and a policeman. Fear pinched her beautiful face.

Great! What now?

Water drizzled down his body and he felt at a distinct disadvantage facing authorities in skimpy swim gear and bare feet. Dreading the confrontation, his heart hammered against his ribs. "Is there a problem, gentlemen?" He eyed each in turn, his gaze stopping on the gray-suited, fiftyish man sporting a bushy handlebar mustache.

"Let's go to my office where we can be more comfortable." The man led the way, his footsteps sharp, his motions jerky. A slight limp punctuated the cadence of his gait.

Nautical décor filled the office, not surprising for the Keys. Fisherman's net draped the ceiling. Life rings, driftwood, and pictures of lighthouses hung on the walls. Behind him, the policeman stood at parade rest like a Buckingham Palace Guard.

The director closed the door with a soft click and then marched behind the huge oak desk neatly stacked with several piles of documents. He stared Eddie in the eye for a long moment. "I'm Dominic Inchitti, director of the aquarium. I must say we have *never* had anything like this happen in my fourteen-year tenure here."

Eddie cleared his throat and shifted to a more comfortable position on his numb legs. "I still don't know what this is all about."

Diana hung her head, her glorious hair hiding her face. She turned away fractionally from him so he couldn't catch a glimpse of her expression. But tension cascaded off her in waves.

"Miss Venus stole one of our rarest fish from our aquariums. She was caught eating it in the hallway outside the aquarium."

The formerly silent lifeguard carried an open box to him that contained a large flat buttercup yellow fish with several chunks bitten out of its body. The bloody view made Eddie turn his head. Sushi was one thing, but this? "Diana?"

She recoiled at her name, but then slowly turned to him and lifted her gaze. Gloomy eyes dominated her pinched face. "I'm sorry. I was so hungry. I don't even remember doing it, it happened so fast..." She spread her arms wide and rotated her palms toward the ceiling. "I didn't know it was against the law. Truly."

Crimson flooded Inchitti's broad cheeks, and he paced the floor with his hands linked behind his back. "Warning signs are posted everywhere. She went into a restricted area. I'm absolutely appalled at this woman's actions."

Diana sat primly, her hands now folded in her lap. She looked up at the furious man. "I'm deeply sorry, but I can't read. I couldn't tell there were warnings."

A frown stole into Eddie's heart. How could a grown woman not be able to read? Not that he could recall her reading or writing, and come to think of it, she shied away from the computer. That was highly unusual for this day and age. The more he learned about her, the more mysterious she seemed. Strange as her actions were, he detected no forethought of malice.

"Clearly she intended no harm. I'll cover your expenses and I'm sure she'll make a formal apology if you won't press charges."

The policeman looked at the director. "It's your call. You have legal grounds, but it seems as if Miss Venus is remorseful and meant no injury and they are willing to pay damages and apologize."

Inchitti leaned heavily on his desk. "If you apologize and make full restitution to the seaquarium we won't press charges. She'll be banned for life, of course, and I'll have to procure another *Holocanthus ciliaris* for the seaquarium."

At Eddie's puzzled look, Inchitti said, "Queen Angelfish. Be warned, Mr. Whatever-your-name-is, it could be costly."

A costly *fish*? *It wasn't large like a dolphin.*

Eddie gulped. At the fast food joint they cost five bucks with fries. But it was settle out of court or Diana could face criminal charges. "We agree."

Diana wrapped her shaky fingers around his wrist. "I didn't know it was wrong to eat a fish…"

Anger and exhaustion brewed up a rotten case of indigestion in his chest. He would help her out of this mess but needed to do some serious thinking about having a relationship with Diana—business or personal. A lot of things didn't add up about her. Despite her ethereal beauty, she might not be a good employee or girlfriend.

* * * * *

What seemed like an eternity and a forest worth of paperwork later, Diana was permitted to leave.

Angry clouds brewed overhead as they emerged into a late afternoon that was growing as gloomy as her mood. A brisk wind blew salty mist off the Atlantic into her face, practically acid to a cat. Rubbing her arms vigorously, she couldn't stop shivering.

What a thoroughly miserable day!

Venus help her!

She had no choice but to reveal her true identity and hope Eddie would accept her. If he truly loved her, it should not matter what or who she was in her former life. Nevertheless, they had traveled in silence for two Keys up the road before she screwed up her courage enough to broach the subject. She cleared her throat. "I can explain."

Of course she could explain, but it would sound like a totally farfetched, unbelievable story.

Eddie's countenance turned stonier if that was possible. He slid a stormy glance at her and his knuckles whitened on the steering wheel. "*Now* you can explain? Isn't it several hours and a few hundred dollars too late? What kind of pussyfooting around are you up to?"

Wincing, her heart sank lower as his outrage and pain washed over her. "I-I needed to tell you this in private."

If she told her story in front of those dour people at the seaquarium, they'd have had her locked away.

When she reached out to him, placing her hand on his arm, he yanked away from her as if burned. Grimacing, she said sadly, "I don't deserve that."

Venus had warned her that humans could feel so much more pain. She had believed her but had no clue just how large human hearts were. How vulnerable.

Scowling, he pulled onto the side of the road and faced her. He leaned against the door as if putting as much distance between them as he possibly could in the cramped vehicle.

"What do you deserve? You hold so much back. I don't know you at all."

His accusation cut her to the core yet she clung to his confession that she had invaded his heart. If there was love, there was hope. If her foolish actions this morning hadn't killed his love for her. Hadn't the goddess warned her not to act on her natural feline instincts that humans wouldn't accept? Distraught, she dragged in a deep breath and clenched her fists. "I was afraid you wouldn't believe me...or accept me."

Eddie sat so near, yet seemed so remote. His gaze didn't falter but his fingers twitched. "I won't know 'til you tell me."

She flicked her hair behind her shoulders, anchoring the long locks behind her ears. The door handle dug into her back so she sat up straighter. "Do you believe in miracles?"

Skepticism crept into his eyes and his brow arched. "What sort of miracles?"

Sucking in a deep breath, her lungs expanded against her ribs as thunder cracked in the distance. "Second chances. Reincarnation."

"I never much thought about it." His gaze skittered across the crashing waves dashing their strip of beach. *Not a good sign.*

She started to knead her lap with her fingernails and stopped. "I was more transformed than reincarnated."

"Transformed? How?" Eddie's eyes narrowed to mere slits.

"I know it's fantastic but I swear on the goddess Venus herself it's the truth." Her heart reverberated with her hope and prayers that he would believe her.

"Venus? The mythological Roman goddess of love?" He gave her a skeptical look.

He didn't believe her.

Swallowing hard, she nodded. "The goddess of love, yes. Mythological, no. She's as real as you and I."

"And I suppose you know because you've met her. In Heaven. She *transformed* you?"

The derision in his voice shattered what was left of her battered heart.

"Yes." How could she provide proof to him, short of introducing him to the goddess? She prayed with all her soul that Venus would materialize and show herself to Eddie, but knew that was impossible.

"If you were transformed, who were you before?" His face a gray mask, his gaze felt cold and disinterested.

This was it. No more stalling. She prayed for Venus' favor and assistance. *Please soften Eddie's heart. Open his mind. Let him believe me.*

"*Diamond*," she said on a loud whisper, her gaze strong on his face. She willed him to believe and accept.

"*A diamond?*" Confusion clouded Eddie's eyes.

"Your pet. Diamond. The cat that saved the neighbor child from the alligator; well, that was me."

Eddie threw a sharp look at her and folded his arms over his chest. Then his gaze narrowed on her. "Do you truly believe this?"

"It's the truth." She leaned forward, the truth giving her courage. "My reward for sacrificing my life was to be granted my deepest desire — to return to the one I love, in a form he could love in return." She couldn't exhale, awaiting his reaction. Her future, their love, her life, depended on his ability to love her and accept the facts.

* * * * *

Paralyzed, Eddie just stared at the vision of insanity in front of him. She had to be psychotic or worse. It was sadistic to claim credit for saving the boy. And he'd brought her into his house and trusted her. The seaquarium's director couldn't know how right he'd been to demand psychiatric care.

Fury simmered in his veins until it exploded into a full boil. How could she look so angelic yet be so demonic?

"Lady, I don't know what drugs you're on, or which ones you're not taking, but you're dangerous. I want you out of my house and my life *tonight*."

"You have to believe me! Everything I told you is true." She grasped his hand between hers and he gazed up into sad amber eyes.

Oh no! He couldn't let himself be sucked in by a beautiful teary-eyed woman.

Almost electrocuted by her touch, he yanked his hand back. "Inchitti's right. You need help. Our neighborhood medical center has a program for this sort of thing. I'll drop you off."

"I'm not delusional. I'm not lying. Reincarnation is real. So is Heaven…"

"And Venus?" This was getting old, not to mention downright weird. Starting the engine, he slipped back into the heavy evening traffic exiting the Keys.

"Why won't you believe me? I love you."

Crazy! Big time.

He closed his ears to her phony pleas. Either she was a nut who truly believed this gibberish, or she was a fraud. He wasn't sure which was worse.

"There's a show on the psychic channel that explains it. We can watch it when we get home."

"I don't buy into that psychic bullshit. They're all con artists on that station." His heart splintering, he punched the dashboard.

What a nightmare!

Chapter Eight

Con artists.

The phrase echoed in her head the remainder of the painfully silent ride home.

Home.

Not hers any longer. He was kicking her out.

She had no place to go, nowhere to turn and no way to earn her keep. Her heart throbbed and her head was so heavy she leaned it against the seat.

She'd be a stray. An alley cat.

When they arrived at the house, two white sedans and a police cruiser filled their driveway making her heart lurch. *What now?* Had the seaquarium changed its mind and decided to press charges after all?

Then Shawna sashayed in front of the vehicles, her smile sickeningly smug, her stance victorious.

Diana's heart lurched.

What was the wicked witch of Florida doing here?

"What the hell?" When Eddie slammed on the brakes, Diana's seat belt almost strangled her.

One woman and two men, one in an FLPD uniform approached the van holding out their badges for inspection.

Eddie rammed the van into park and alighted from the vehicle. "Stay here, Diam...Diana," he practically growled.

Was he beginning to believe her? Hope mingled with fear. Not eager to face her fate, but having nowhere else to go, she remained in her seat.

The policeman strolled to her side of the vehicle. "Would you step out, please ma'am?"

Eddie motioned for her to get out of the van.

"We'd like to talk to you inside, Miss Venus. Come with us please," the man said as he held the door for her.

Shawna shot her a wickedly superior glance and then pranced into the house at Eddie's side. The other woman clutched his forearm as if she owned him.

A growl rumbled deep in Diana's stomach and her fingers curled. How she missed her claws and her flesh-tearing fangs. Without them, she felt completely defenseless.

When her escorts closed the door behind them, she felt trapped. "Have a seat," the man said, inclining his head at the long couch.

Eddie leaned against the computer desk, lightning raging in his eyes.

Shawna perched on the chair not even a cat's length from him. Putting her hand proprietarily on Eddie's forearm, she grinned widely in Diana's direction.

Jealousy gnawed at her insides when Eddie didn't remove the hand or take exception to Shawna's advances. He didn't seem to mind his assistant taking such liberties.

"We're here because Miss Moran reported that you're an illegal alien."

Diana gasped, appalled at the woman's viciousness, and sank onto the loveseat. Would she go to any length to win Eddie's affections?

Rosie crawled into Diana's lap and rubbed her fluffy head against Diana's hands, lending comfort. The kitten meowed up at her with troubled eyes, pleading, "Don't leave me, Auntie Diamond."

Not to be outdone, Napoleon curled up on her feet, between her and the threatening intruders. A low growl rumbled in his chest and Diana nudged him gently, warning him to stay calm.

"Are you policemen, too?" Tearing her gaze from Shawna's malevolent one, she studied the strangers in regular clothing. The man wore a tanned suit similar to that of Mr. Inchitti at the seaquarium. Asexual with her red hair scraped severely away from her too thin face, the woman looked like a matchstick wearing a stuffy black suit. They presented their credentials to her with robotic motions.

"She doesn't read," Eddie said as if in explanation, his voice deadpan.

Shawna snorted and batted her false lashes at the detectives. "Everybody can read — except maybe illegal aliens."

She was learning how to read! But she thought better of offering that bit of information. They might twist it around so that it would be of more harm than good.

The man answered and nodded. "We're with the INS." When Diana gave them a blank stare, the woman supplied, "Immigration and Naturalization Services. I'm Agent Amanda Carrolle and my partner is Agent Tad Foley. We investigate reports of people who are in the US without authorization."

"I was born in Florida. I've lived here all my life." Diana began to relax, the knots in her muscles unfurling. They thought she had come from somewhere else.

"Perhaps this is just a misunderstanding. If you'll just produce your driver's license, social security card, or birth certificate, we'll check it and be on our way."

Panic assailed again her full force and her lungs threatened to collapse. *Oh, Venus! Why didn't you give me these things? Please help me!*

But her prayers went unheeded. Of course. Venus had warned her about revealing herself. No papers floated down from the sky. No documentation magically appeared in her pocket.

Stall. The word popped into her brain as she opened her mouth to admit she had no such documents. "I-I misplaced them. I'll have to find them."

"She suffers from amnesia," Eddie said, shocking her. He stood tall, his expression rapt on her.

Playing along, she hoped the officers would believe her, although she'd learned to her chagrin that humans were a very skeptical species.

"I lost my memory." The words rang false in her ears and for once, she wished she had cultivated the human trait of lying.

"How extremely convenient," Shawna drawled, rolling her eyes. "If you can't remember, how do you know you were born here or lived here all your life? Hmm… Sounds fishy to me."

Diana tried to take her own advice and remain calm. She petted the purring Rosie as she tried to breathe evenly.

Eddie walked away from Shawna at that and sat on the couch beside Diana. Thankfully he ignored the petulant troublemaker's sniff. She felt better surrounded by her loved ones. United, they stood a better chance of victory.

"Have you reported her as a missing person to the police?" Foley asked sharply. "Is she under a doctor's care?"

"Noooo." Eddie tensed beside her even as he remained affable to the officer. "I just discovered this. I was going to report it…"

"I love your selective memory," Shawna drawled sarcastically, strolling over to the group and perched on the arm of the couch next to Eddie who scowled deeply.

"Does she have to be here?" Disgust filled Diana's heart when she looked at the witch who was worse than the alligator who had devoured her.

"She makes some good points," Agent Carrolle said, pacing behind her partner, her eyes calculating. "It's obvious Miss Venus requires medical treatment and observation. It's my opinion that this case warrants further investigation."

Diana's stomach flip-flopped and she felt as if she was going to cough up a hairball. But then Eddie wanted her out of his house and his life anyway, so did it really matter where she went? Venus had obviously deserted her.

"Please accompany us, Miss Venus," Foley said.

Rosie climbed onto Diana's shoulder and hugged her. "You can't go."

Heaven knew she didn't want to, but it seemed she had no choice.

Eddie jumped to his feet, facing off against the stoic agent. "Where are you taking her? Doesn't she need a change of clothing?"

"What clothes? She has none, remember?" Shawna said in a dulcet tone, glee flashing in her eyes.

Napoleon bristled against her, his attention riveted on the vile woman. He rose to his feet and stood dangerously still. The dog's promise to protect her flashed across her mind just as he growled again and bared his teeth.

Rosie's fur prickled and she leaped to the back of the couch and disappeared under the protective furniture. She hated it when Napoleon growled.

Before she could stop him, the dog leapt at Shawna and sank his fangs into the meaty flesh of her ankle. She howled in fury and her face turned a bright crimson. Cursing loudly, she kicked at him frantically. "Get this mangy mutt off me before he tears my leg apart!"

The policeman rose to his feet. "Call off your dog, Mr. Davis."

"Napoleon, down! Get off her!" When the dog ignored Eddie, he grabbed him around his middle and yanked him off forcefully.

Shawna glared at Eddie and the dog as she bent down and held her foot. "Get that—that evil thing far away from me. Is the mangy thing up to date on its rabies shots?"

Scowling, Eddie opened the sliding glass door and put Napoleon outside. "I don't know what got into you, boy."

Napoleon barked, trying to tell him what was wrong, but Diana was sure she was the only one who understood what he was saying. He'd been standing up for her. Taking revenge on her behalf. When no one was looking her way except the dog who had his nose pressed against the window, she saluted him and mouthed a silent "thank you".

Napoleon tilted his head at her as if to say "you're welcome" and then bounded to the far end of the fenced yard.

"I'm afraid we'll have to call animal control." The policeman walked toward the back door where Napoleon had been put outside. He spoke lowly into his radio.

Eddie stared at the uniformed man. "I can provide proof of his license and immunization records. He's up on all his shots."

"It's standard procedure. The law says you have to be able to keep control of your animals." The policeman hooked his radio back onto his belt.

Oh no!

She should have held onto Napoleon's collar when he first growled. She could have prevented this.

Shawna glared up at Eddie from her crouched position. Puffy and bruised, her ankle looked to be a mess. "I'll be maimed for life. The least you can do is carry me to the couch and pay my doctor bills."

Eddie scooped the snake into his arms and did her bidding, much to Diana's distaste. So only Napoleon was going to champion her? Eddie seemed much more concerned about the vile woman than her desperate plight.

When Shawna was settled, she narrowed her eyes at the agent in charge. "So, isn't that strange? That woman had no clothing. Nothing. What are you people going to do about it?"

"It's typical for amnesia victims not to have extra clothes," Carrolle said.

Diana smiled, glad the agent had cut her off before she could spout that she had a wardrobe full of clothing now that Eddie had bought for her. Shawna's barb had backfired and might help her. She would have to remember to thank her later for her help. The devil would love that.

"We're going to take Miss Venus with us."

"And what are you going to do about that mangy mutt?" Shawna jerked a finger at the back door where Napoleon pressed his nose, baring his teeth at her.

"Animal control is on the way. They'll handle the matter from here."

"How do I know you called them?"

A knock sounded on the door and the policeman nodded to Eddie to answer it.

With lightning flashing in his eyes, Eddie marched to the door and opened it. "Yeah?"

"Animal control. We had a call to pick up a vicious dog."

Napoleon wasn't vicious! He was only protecting her!

But they were going to lock her away, too, so they'd never listen to her. Right. Like they'd believe her when she told them Napoleon had promised to help her out.

"Well, I disagree that he's vicious, but he's out back. I'm the owner. Will up-to-date medical records and license make a difference?"

"That's not up to me," the animal control representative said, shifting his weight from foot to foot. "My instructions are to take the animal to the Animal Control office. You'll have to discuss that with the director."

More directors! Heaven save them!

The policeman stepped forward. "I called for you. The animal is out back. I witnessed the attack."

"I want that dangerous dog put away where he can't hurt anyone else!" Shawna puffed out her chest and pointed at her injury. "He did this to me."

The animal control agent nodded commiseratively. "You should go to the emergency room to have that examined. Dog bites can be nasty business."

"Okay, Miss Venus. It's time for us to go, too." Miss Carrolle strolled over and stood before her. "Come with me, please.

Diana's heart ached. She had failed miserably all the way around. "Where are you taking me?"

"To our holding center's medical facility in Miami. We'll have more questions for you, don't worry. Now if you'll excuse us." She nodded at the police officer who stepped forward and flanked her.

Fear catapulted through Diana's veins. What if she never saw her family again? What were they going to do to Napoleon? "Eddie! I love you. Help us!" The cry born in her heart shattered her soul. She reached out to him but the agents blocked him. They wouldn't let her say so much as goodbye to Napoleon or Rosie, either.

* * * * *

Help us! echoed in Eddie's head until it drove him insane.

Diana, or Diamond, or whoever the hell she was, loved him. Truth rang in her words. Had he ever doubted that truth? Her kisses didn't lie. Or her gentleness. Someone who could be so tender and loving couldn't be evil.

Hard as he tried, he couldn't sleep. Diana's ghost haunted the house and in particular his bed. It didn't matter which bed he tried to sleep in. Everything reminded him of his lover and taunted him with its emptiness.

He ambled to the computer. Compelled, he pulled up information on reincarnation. Never a believer before, he became fascinated with the possibility.

However, Diana was plainly a grown woman and Diamond had died barely a month before. Clearly Diana had not had time to be reborn and grow to womanhood.

Her explanation that she had been transformed was beginning to make more and more sense. But if the Roman gods were still around, why did no one else speak of them in the present tense? Why were they hiding from people and only showing themselves to cats?

When he next looked outside, the sun shimmered like a sorbet on the horizon. Too late to go to sleep, he suppressed a yawn and ambled down to his darkroom and developed the seaquarium photographs. He grunted in satisfaction at how well they had turned out. Diana was just as photogenic now as his Diamond had been. Several of these shots would make for a great magazine cover.

When nine a.m. rolled around, he made an appointment with a famous past-life psychotherapist in Miami to discuss regression.

Chapter Nine

Diamond hated being caged in the antiseptic clinic with doctors probing her mind, body, and spirit. She knew so little compared to the rest of humanity. The more she learned, the more she discovered she didn't know. Not just reading and academics such as math, but everyday common knowledge like basic health care and societal issues.

She knelt down on her knees and prayed to her goddess. "Dear Venus, please deliver me. Rescue me from this fate. If Eddie doesn't want me as a woman, change me back to a cat to live out my days. Have mercy on me."

Light shimmered in the dark room, startling her. Her hands went to her throat and she backed up against her bed until her knees buckled and she fell backward. She breathed a sigh of relief when the goddess's shape solidified and her smile radiated over her.

"Rise, little one, and come over here."

Diana obeyed and stopped a pace in front of her patron. "It is as you warned it might be. I'm unable to pass for a human female. I can't make the change. My master doesn't love me as I love him." Why, oh why, hadn't the goddess warned her not to eat fish raw, either?

"I warned you what would happen if you erred again. To be human brings greater joy but also greater woe and responsibility. I'd hoped you'd be able to make the adjustment but it seems that isn't so."

An older being with a long white flowing beard and hair appeared beside the goddess. "Daughter, I trust this latest project of yours won't become the talk of the land. Your penchant for transforming creatures worries me."

"But, Father, no one knows but you, me, and Diana." The goddess gazed up at her father with pleading eyes.

"And the human male upon whom she has designs. And your brother. Who do you think told me?" Venus's father raised his chin regally and glared down his patrician nose at her.

"Excuse me," Diana said, awestruck to be in the god's presence. "What can I do? I don't fit into either world. The humans won't accept me as one of theirs." She looked around the strange room with the shiny silver surfaces covered by vials of liquids and cluttered with several snowy starched beds. It would be a blessing if Venus changed her back to her true form.

Venus smiled upon her benignly. "I know what you've been going through. Have faith a little while longer, my pet."

"She is no longer *your pet*!" Jupiter bellowed, his beard bobbing over his barrel chest. "She is a woman. I hope you know what you're doing."

Venus rolled her eyes at her sire's back. "I'm thirty-one-thousand years old. Give me a little credit, Father."

The god snorted and stroked his beard. "What a romantic creature you are, my daughter. No one else in the galaxy sees things as you do. Only you would dream that a human woman would kiss a frog, or a human man might fall in love with a cat."

A strangled cry gurgled up in Diana's throat. She tried to choke back the hot tears scalding the backs of her eyes as her heart plummeted to her knees.

The god's expression softened and he laid a hand on Diana's shoulder. "Sorry, my dear. That was unforgivably insensitive of me."

Diana tried to smile but it wavered on her lips as if pulled down by her heavy heart. "I need your help if I'm ever to be released from this prison. I don't have the papers Eddie's government requires."

"Ah, yes. Mortals of this era are overly attached to their red tape. They were much more fun in ancient Rome, before computers were invented."

"I wouldn't say that too loudly." A wry smile twisted the goddess's lips. "Minerva is particularly fond of her newest inspiration and you can't charm her the way I let you charm me."

Jupiter waved his hand in the air dismissively. "Bother the egghead. She was a computer geek before computers were invented. Before this it was the calculator, slide rule, and the abacus."

"What about me?" Diana didn't fit into this human world even as well as an egghead or a geek.

"You still have a few months until the enchantment wears off. If Edward truly loves you, he will find a way to keep you."

"But I want to be restored to my feline state. I can't live with this human heartache any longer."

"You have too little faith. Give it time." The gods smiled and disappeared in a twinkling fog.

"Wait!" Mumbling to herself as she perched on the windowsill, she tucked her knees beneath her chin. She gazed unseeingly upon the moon and stars twinkling above her. "I'll never get out of here if I tell the doctors my goddess is working on my escape plan."

Better than confessing she was once a cat.

* * * * *

A small ball of energy rushed into the office, the doctor's arms loaded with technical manuals and case studies. "Nice to meet you. I'm Dr. André Mazato." Thick lips protruded from the mass of gray beard that contrasted with his shiny, bald pate. His platinum-plated watch and black suit seemed incongruous with his long, straggly ponytail.

"So what is it you hope to gain by probing your past lives?" The man dumped his load haphazardly onto the cluttered desk, and then leaned over the mess to shake hands.

"I'm on a fact-finding mission for a friend, rather than here for myself." Eddie cracked his knuckles one by one, something he hadn't done since he'd been a school kid in the principal's office.

Mazato nodded as he shrugged out of his jacket and flung it over his coat rack. Then he hitched up his slacks and lowered himself into an overstuffed recliner that topped his head by half a foot. Unbuttoning his sleeves, he rolled them back, revealing springy graying hair on his scrawny arms. "Tell me about your *friend*."

"She claims she was a cat in a past life. That's not possible, is it? Is she psychotic?" Eddie teetered on the edge of a buttery soft leather couch as he stared at two full walls of degrees, certifications, and awards wondering if they were real or facsimiles.

"It is not only possible, but probable. Each of us possesses an intricate thread of previous beings within our experience. Let me illustrate the therapeutic potential by taking you back and introducing you to one of your former selves."

Still skeptical, Eddie massaged the back of his neck. "How will I know you aren't just making this up to get my bank account numbers while I'm under your spell?"

"I'm board-certified and of course you're most welcome to check out my credentials. My pristine reputation is invaluable to me. I would not jeopardize it to steal personal information. However..." The psychologist scribbled notes on his pad, loosened his tie, then pushed a button on a portable tape player before settling back against the chair with a smile. "It might make you feel better to know I tape every regressive session."

Eddie stretched his fingers, still uncertain whether or not to be regressed, but he tried to relax. He could just buy that astral software he'd found online for $19.95 instead of shelling out a couple hundred bucks to a charlatan. "How will I know what you reveal is true, and not just the result of a hypnotic suggestion? Will I remember any of it?"

"Yes. It will be as if a light is illuminating the darkness. But I must warn you, however, that you may not like all you discover about your past lives. One or more could be less than honorable and not necessarily human."

"I won't start quacking like a duck or mooing like a cow?" Or meowing like a cat? If he started howling like a wolf he was out of here.

"Of course not. Even if one of your former lives was as another species that doesn't mean you're that species presently. You won't be compelled to do anything you wouldn't normally do. This is merely therapy to help you heal and progress so you can get on with this life."

"Does that mean I'll become a god someday if I progress enough?" He thought it a fair question. If this reincarnation stuff was true, didn't that mean that beings kept doing things over until they were perfect? What was more perfect than god-dom?

He chuckled at his own absurdity. He couldn't believe he was seriously considering this nonsense. Still, a small shred of doubt prevented him from walking out. He'd battled Miami rush hour traffic to get here, so he might as well see it through. Few things in any lifetime were as scary as the main highway during rush hour. "Okay, let's do it. I hope I wasn't a girl."

"We often change genders from life to life. In one life you may be the husband and in the next, your former wife will be your husband."

Great.

"So, Doc, why do most people come to see you? They can't all have women friends swearing they were a cat at one time."

A smile played on the counselor's lips. "Not that I can divulge specifics but most of my patients need healing. They suffer effects of unresolved issues from former lives. They can't progress until they confront and overcome their pasts."

He was already here, so he might as well give it a chance. "I'm game. So now what? Do I lie down and put up my feet?"

"We'll start with light hypnosis. This will help you remember what you've seen." The older man rechecked the recorder, then picked up a silver pocket watch and let the chain slide through his fingers until the fob dangled before Eddie's face.

Stars glinted from the shiny object, fascinating Eddie. His reflection regarded him, his face too broad and long. Small and beady, his eyes stared back at him. Distorted as the image was, it still looked better than his God-awful driver's license photo.

A flick of the doctor's wrist sent the disc spinning. "Focus on the watch. Don't remove your gaze from it. Picture yourself coming down a long staircase. When you reach the bottom, you'll see two doors and a couch. One door will be red. Do you see it?"

Eddie felt weird, as if floating, yet he could still feel the leather couch beneath him. The red door seemed to zoom up on him, large, glowing, and vibrating. "Yes. I see it."

"Good. Open that door and enter. There will be a long corridor. At the end is another door." The doctor's soothing voice droned in his head, mesmerizing him.

He struggled through a mist, traversing a dark, narrow hallway. His palms grew clammy as his footsteps rang out hollowly. The hallway loomed longer than it had first appeared, as if it was an optical illusion. "What's behind the second door?"

"One of your past lives. The memory you most need to see at this point in your present existence to resolve the issue which needs healing."

Eddie seemed to be having trouble keeping his eyes open despite his sudden incapability to blink. He was aware of everything, though his attention remained riveted on the spinning timepiece. The doctor hooked the watch fob onto some sort of metal tree sculpture, and then laced his hands together on top of the desk, flexing his fingers.

The door loomed before Eddie and he hesitated in front of it, his breathing raspy, his chest tight. What if he opened the door to a monster? To a hostile world? Some people claimed you could die from extreme fright inside a dream. Was this any different?

"Have you reached the door yet?" The doctor's rich baritone echoed in his mind, pushing him onward.

"Yes."

"Good. Open it, nice and slow, and then stand on the threshold. Just look inside and tell me what you see." The doctor lowered his voice to a whisper.

Eddie hardly dared to breathe and could feel the whir of the tape recorder in his bones. His blood simmered in his veins and his pulse throbbed as he reached for the door.

Slowly, he opened it and stepped forward so that he stood on the verge of a beautifully lush forest. Fireflies flitted around a meadow cascading with blue bonnets and daffodils.

"Describe what you see."

He peered closer, unable to believe his own senses. Those tiny winged creatures weren't fireflies! "Fairies are flying around a field of flowers. And there are unicorns, dragons, and gryphons."

"Are there any other beings present?"

Eddie squinted into the waning sun of dusk, letting his gaze roam as far as he could see. At the edge of the glade he spied a big, burly black and white tomcat crouching as if ready to pounce. Then a second white cat, smaller than the first, joined him. Obviously happy to see the newcomer, the first cat rubbed against her and then they frolicked in the meadow chasing butterflies. "Yes, two cats. Male and female, I think."

"Does any particular creature capture your attention?" The man's words flowed seamlessly into the sounds of the forest— birds chirping, the soft breeze rustling in the long, waving grass, horses whinnying softly to their mates, and the cats' meowing to each other sounded loudest of all.

"The tomcat." The creature's coat looked like a tuxedo with a solid black back. A long, white stripe ran up his belly to fan out on his snowy-white neck. He also noticed that the creature had abnormally large paws with an extra finger—a polydactyl like Diamond had been. Could it be that he focused on the tomcat because he had cats on the brain? Or because the man put a hypnotic suggestion in his mind?

"Good. Good. We're getting somewhere. Now, I want you to walk closer to the cat and sit down. Just observe for a few more minutes."

Eddie nodded, feeling strangely as if he was in two places at once. He strolled into the glade, trying not to make a sound that would frighten away the creatures. Several fairies pointed at him and giggled, their tinkling laughter sweet and joyful. Wraithlike, their tiny wings glittered and glowed. He felt like Gulliver in the land of the Lilliputians. Except that the cats seemed their ordinary size.

A unicorn ambled up to him and nudged him with its horn. Lavender eyes peered at him curiously as the creature tossed its lilac mane and snorted at him. Maybe he had been the unicorn. That would be cool—if he couldn't be human. "Was I you?"

The unicorn sniffed him up and down, and then shook its head. "Not I. Your first instinct was the correct one."

The tomcat...

"How do you know?" Eddie's glance slid to the cats that were now making slow, languorous love on a bed of clovers. The tomcat humped the female as she screamed in ecstasy.

Eddie tore his gaze away from the scene, turning his attention again to the unicorn. He opened his mouth to speak, but the creature knew his question before he could form it.

"How do I speak to you? How do I see into your past and your future? I'm magical." Its sparkling tail thrashed and he neighed. Pivoting on his back hooves, he galloped away in the opposite direction and then leaped into the mist.

The sound of mating cats drew Eddie's attention again. Awe filled his heart. "I was a cat." But that wasn't the only revelation dawning on him. The white female cat was none other than Diamond—Diana. They had been together before, had loved before.

A smile dawned over the doctor's face and he sat up straight and stroked his beard. "How does this make you feel?"

Strangely enough, joy swelled in his heart as he watched the felines perform the ancient dance of love. Warmth suffused him and his toes tingled as they rolled together in the field. "Fantastic."

"Free? Enlightened? Ready to open your mind to the possibility that your woman friend is telling the truth?" Either the doctor was a sorcerer or a mind reader to know all this.

"I'm going to snap my fingers on the count of three and you will return to normal. You will remember everything." The doctor counted slowly but concisely and then snapped his fingers in Eddie's face, awakening him.

Eddie jerked back to reality, yet he had perfect recollection of the past hour's events. "I knew Diana before. We were lovers."

A frown tugged at his lips and he stretched out his legs before him. "I was a cat, too."

"Yes. It would appear so. I was once a bull elephant in the jungles of Africa. In another life, I was a belly dancer in a sheik's harem."

"No one famous?"

"The nearest I ever came to fame was when I was a foot soldier in the Pharaoh's army in ancient Egypt—the ones Moses drowned when he brought the waters of the Red Sea crashing down upon us. Few of us were famous people, because the truth is, considering the sheer number of lives past, there have been few famous people in the history of the world. The odds would be more than a billion to one."

"May I ask a question, Doc?" Eddie scratched his cheek, trying to figure out how to put it. Seeing Diana—rather, Diamond—back there in the glade gave him a lot to ponder.

"Shoot." The doctor picked up a Rubik's Cube on the corner of his desk and fiddled with it, his gaze still rapt on Eddie.

"Do we always have the same lovers? Friends? From life to life?"

"There is a theory that we each have a core group that travels with us through time. It is my belief that our soul mates keep reappearing in our lives as well as a few other close friends and family, yes. My wife's been with me for tens of thousands of years. Of course, sometimes she's the husband and I'm the wife. Or concubine." A naughty smile danced in his eyes.

"I have a lot to think about." Like finding Diana and apologizing.

Mazato stood and rounded the desk. "I'd be delighted to regress you again in another session, or speak more about this one. Stop by my receptionist on your way out to arrange another appointment."

"Thanks, Doc. I'll let you know if I think it's necessary." Eddie rose to his full height, nearly a head taller than the distinguished man. His shadow eclipsed the other man's and he felt like a giant again. Antsy, he couldn't wait to find Diana and tell her everything that had just transpired.

Then he would get his dog back.

Chapter Ten

Diana awakened with a jerk, curled into a ball on an unfamiliar bed, her arm lying over her head. Disoriented, she looked around to get her bearings. It didn't look like the pound, yet she was locked in a cold, barren room from which there was no escape.

When memory rushed in on her, she moaned. She was still incarcerated in the INS medical clinic. It might as well be the pound like poor Napoleon. At least at the pound, someone might come to adopt her. Here, they would try to deport her, even though she had nowhere to go. What country would want her with no known past, nor any papers? Did they put humans to sleep?

Oh God! They wouldn't put Napoleon to sleep, would they? He'd only been trying to protect her.

Wide awake now, she couldn't sit still so she prowled around the room, peeking into cupboards and drawers that were all empty.

Oh, Venus! Am I being punished? I thought I was supposed to endure.

She wandered over to the window and curled up on the ledge again. The dawning sun was just beginning to warm it and she leaned her head against the cool glass. She longed for freedom, to feel the grass under her feet, the wind in her hair and Eddie's strong arms holding her securely. She even longed to see the dog again, running free in the backyard barking his head off, bringing the neighbor's wrath down upon them.

The door clicked open but she didn't turn around. It must be a nurse that wanted to check her temperature again. She couldn't work up any enthusiasm to see another stranger.

Strangers.

Two sets of footsteps closed in on her. One female. One male. She could hear the difference in the cadence and the heaviness. Human females pranced or glided. Overflowing with testosterone, human males swaggered. This one definitely swaggered.

"You have a visitor, Diana," a soft feminine voice said. She recognized it as belonging to the night nurse.

She caught wind of Eddie's beloved scent, and her heart lurched against her ribs. Whirling around, she almost fell off her precarious seat. "Eddie! You came. I was afraid that you'd never want to see me again." Euphoria pushing out the despair, she rushed into his embrace, and buried her face against his rapidly beating heart.

Eddie's darkened gaze stole her breath. He caught her to him and swung her around. "I wasn't sure I was going to come, either."

The import of his words stung. He wasn't happy to see her? She pulled away and gazed deeply into his eyes, wishing she could look into his heart. "You weren't?" She choked on her words, but held her head high, holding back tears with all her might.

"I wasn't. But then I had a change of heart."

The young nurse backed away, veiling her eyes with her lashes. Twin rose petals colored her cheeks. "I'll be just outside the door if you need me."

"You did?" Her lips felt suddenly parched and she sucked the bottom one into her mouth and chewed it.

"Yes." He looked about as uncomfortable as she felt. He plunged his hands deep into his jeans pockets and then looked heavenward. "Uh, I believe you now."

"You do?" Watching him warily, she couldn't tell if he was happy about his newfound belief.

He closed the gap between them and captured her hands in his, rubbing her knuckles with the pads of his thumbs. "I do. I did a lot of research on reincarnation and even consulted a past-life psychotherapist who showed me one of my past lives."

She let her pent-up breath whoosh out in relief. "You had a past life, too?" His thumbs continued working their magic on her and she let him pull her back to him.

"Um-hmm." He ground his hips against hers, instantly sparking the flame in her womb. "I sure did. Supposedly, we all have several of them. Something about working out problems until we get it right and progress."

"So you believe me now? Can you accept the fact I was a cat?" She could hardly breathe with him rubbing against her. A slow burn moved up her body as he leaned even closer so that his chest rubbed hers.

"I can and I do." He licked her neck with a slow, languorous sweep of his tongue.

She moaned and arched herself closer to him, wishing they were home and alone in the privacy of their bedroom so she could show him just how ecstatic she was about his revelation.

He swirled his tongue in her ear, and let his hands roam her body, practically bringing her to orgasm. He whispered huskily, "I have a confession."

"Which is?" She closed her eyes and gave herself up to the wonderful sensations cascading through her.

"I was a cat, too. And you were my mate."

She opened one eye to peer at him. "For real?"

He crossed his heart. "I swear it's the truth. The unicorn said so."

"Unicorn? Aren't they mythical creatures?" He had to be teasing her. All the learning channels on TV claimed they were fabled creatures.

He grabbed her hand and coaxed her to turn back to him. "I'm not making this up. I went to a regressionist and I spoke to a unicorn in my past life."

She tilted her head and studied his expression for any nuance of mirth or insincerity.

"You believe in your goddess, right?"

Of course she did!

She nodded. "Venus is as real as you and I. It is because of her that I stand here now."

"So is my unicorn. Well, he's not *my* unicorn, but he's real all the same." Eddie's hair tumbled over his eyes and he looked so adorable she could eat him up. If only he wasn't making fun of her.

"So why are you here? Really? I want the truth."

"I told you. I believe you."

"You came all this way at the crack of dawn to tell me you believe me?" She linked her hands behind her back and swayed her hips. The sun of the new day warmed her and she reveled in it, but not nearly so much as she reveled in his confession.

He dug in his pocket and dragged out a velvet box. Holding it out to her, he cleared his throat, and said in a gruff voice, "Well, I also have a very important question for you."

At sight of the blue velvet ring-size box, she couldn't breathe. This is how men proposed in all the soap operas. Her heart in her throat, she sought his gaze.

Love glowing in his eyes, he lowered himself to bended knee and held it up to her. Then he opened it to reveal a beautiful gold band with one large diamond in the center surrounded by two smaller ones on each side.

She gasped, her hands clutching her throat as she stared from the beautiful expression of his love to him.

"Marry me, Diana. I want us be together eternally, as we're meant to be." Emotion resonated in his voice.

Despite the joy flooding her heart, she burned to know what had become of his hateful assistant. "What about Shawna? You don't love her?" She held her breath, watching him closely, praying he would say no.

Eddie squinted up at her. "Shawna? Where'd you get that idea? She was only my assistant. She's not even that now."

Why did humans have to speak in so many riddles? "What happened to her?" Twinges of conscience gave her pause. She hoped the woman hadn't been seriously injured by Napoleon, even if she didn't care for her. "She didn't get seriously ill from the dog bite, did she?"

Eddie brushed the back of her hand with his lips, making her feel very cherished and special so that she wished she could still purr. "Luckily it was just superficial. She blew it way out of proportion, and then tried to take me to the cleaners. I fired her for that but mostly for the way she tried to get you into trouble. Believe me, we're well rid of her. She's long gone."

Eddie truly loved her! He had championed her. Love swelled in her heart and she flung herself into his arms, bowling him backward onto the ground. "Yes!" She plundered him with kisses as he slipped the token of his love on her engagement finger.

Then reality sobered her and she sat away from him, crossing her legs. "I'd love to marry you, but how can I? I have no documents to prove who I am. I can't even get out of here."

Documents floated onto her lap and then Venus shimmered into the room beside her. "Didn't I tell you to have faith, my pet?"

Eddie did a double take and stared slack-jawed at the goddess. "Is she…"

Diana nodded and drew herself to her feet beside her patron. "Yes. This is Venus."

"I heard you before, Eddie." The goddess tsk-tsked at him, laughing out loud. "I'm as real as your friend, the unicorn."

Diana stared at the papers that had fallen into her hands and was able to read a few words. That television set was a marvelous invention. The morning children's shows had taught her the alphabet and she could spell some simple words. But she didn't understand most of the long, intimidating words on this document. With work and practice, she promised herself she'd learn. For now, she held them out to Eddie for help. "Are these what I hope they are?"

A slow smile dawned over Eddie's face as he flipped through the sheaf of papers. "Yep. Looks like you're official now."

"Those are your copies certifying that you are a bona fide citizen of this country. I personally placed the original documents in their proper government agency files. You're legal now."

Squealing her delight, Diana hugged Venus tightly. "Thank you. Thank you! You won't be sorry you did this."

"I'll never be sorry I helped you. You have proven your worthiness time and again." Venus snapped her fingers. "Oh! I almost forgot. I have another surprise for you."

Another one?

"Napoleon's back home and he's a free dog. I wiped out all record, all memories about his unfortunate incident and I fixed Ms. Moran's ankle." Venus showed an image of the dog in Eddie's room, happily chewing on his new slippers.

Oops!

Diana slanted a glance at Eddie and breathed a sigh of relief when a huge grin split his face.

"Am I allowed to kiss a goddess?" Eddie opened his arms and stepped forward.

"You have my permission." Laughter danced in the goddess' eyes as she presented her cheek to Eddie.

Eddie pecked the beautiful being on her cheek, and then returned to Diana's side.

Radiance glowing on her face, Venus said, "These are my wedding gifts to you."

"These are the best gifts in the world." She could be with Eddie forever now. Eternally grateful to Venus, her heart swelling with love, she hugged her fiercely.

"Be happy together. I have to get back. You'll be fine now. Just tell Agent Foley that you found her documents and all will be well. Don't mention anything about the dog or Ms. Moran's ankle."

"Wait!" Alarm almost strangled the word in Diana's throat. Venus couldn't just abandon her. "Will I ever see you again?"

Venus tilted her head and smiled. "For sure. Oh! I almost forgot to tell you that I have another present for you."

Yet another present?

Eddie, her papers, and Napoleon's freedom were presents enough. Still her natural curiosity got the best of her. She had to be extra careful. She didn't have nine lives anymore. Not even eight. "What is it?"

"The Wildlife and Fresh Fish Commission caught your alligator—with a little help from your favorite goddess. I thought you'd like to know so you can be at peace."

Sighs of relief whooshed out of Diana and Eddie simultaneously, and then they laughed. What huge weights had been lifted from her shoulders.

"This is better than Christmas," Eddie said, putting a possessive arm around Diana's waist and drawing her against him. He didn't protest a bit when she snuggled closer.

"Thank you for everything." Diana blinked back a tear, feeling silly, as the goddess had promised they would meet again.

"Ditto," Eddie said, squeezing Diana gently.

"Ciao!" The goddess winked and then faded into nothingness.

Eddie moved Diana aside gently and stuck his hand through the goddess' shimmering haze, examining it intently. "Guess it's not a parlor trick. I wouldn't have believed it if I hadn't seen it."

Unsure if he was committing a sacrilege or not, she shivered, and yanked it out. "Be careful! She could turn you into a toad." She remembered how Apollo had accused his sister of turning a prince into an amphibian.

Eddie rubbed his stubbled chin and shook his head. "So we're not delusional?"

Giddy with happiness, Diana tilted her head as she slipped her arms around his waist and molded herself to him. "Not at all."

She couldn't help chuckling at his most adorable boyish pout even as the sight of his powerful chest made her blood boil. She kissed his neck. He was so tasty she couldn't resist savoring him. She trailed her lips down his chest, unbuttoning his shirt and pushing it out of her way.

Eddie tensed beneath her and put his hands on her shoulders. "Someone's bound to walk in and catch us." He grinned wolfishly at her, igniting another fire in her womb. "Keep that up and we'll never get any work done."

She traced his lips with the tip of her tongue, starved to lick something even tastier. "Take me home, and we'll find out."

"Promises, promises." He brushed her lips with his and murmured, "What are we waiting for? We can be home in forty-five minutes."

Forty-five minutes? Eternity!

Eager to get home and be alone with him, she put her paw—*hand*—in his. Slanting a flirtatious look up at him, she tugged him behind her. She'd eventually get used to thinking in human terms. She'd come so far she couldn't let herself slide back now. "Come on, lover."

Eddie's obsidian eyes glowed and he squeezed her fingers. "We'll be home soon."

They reached home a couple hours later and Eddie crushed her to him as soon as they closed the front door of the house. His lips a mere breath away, he ground out, "God, woman, but you'd tempt a saint."

His strong heartbeat pulsed against her breast and she rubbed against him, her anger dissipating in the face of all-consuming desire. Lifting her lips so that they just brushed his, she murmured against them, "Are you a saint?"

A growl tore from him as he cupped her buttocks in his hands and pulled her incredibly, impossibly closer against his enticing heat. "Not even close." He plundered her lips, drinking deeply. His hands crept beneath her shirt and he massaged her cheeks.

Perfect. Saints sounded boring. Heat enflamed her, almost burning her up, so much more intense than any desire she'd experienced in her former life. Parting her mouth wide, opening herself heart and soul to him, she drank as deeply of him as he did of her.

Swooping her into his arms, he cradled her against his chest and carried her upstairs to his bedroom — *their bedroom.* "I hope your engine's still running."

"Positively racing." She curled her arms around his neck and pressed against him. She licked his neck, loving his taste.

Moaning, he lowered her reverently to the bed and pushed her bottoms down around her ankles and she kicked them off. "We'll never get any work done if you keep that up. Then we'd starve."

Returning the favor, she lowered his slacks, letting her hungry gaze drink in the sight of him. When he scooted closer on the bed, his aroused cock rubbed against her pussy, stimulating her juices, making her writhe.

"Oh, no, we wouldn't." Not in any way that mattered. She spread her legs wider, encircled his cock in her fingers, and pulled it to her hungry cunt.

With a primal grunt, Eddie thrust his length into her, slipping in and out, driving her mad. Sleek and gorgeous, he was a powerful tiger. And so devilishly dangerous...

Shuddering in ecstasy, she lifted her hips high, matching his frantic rhythm, meeting him thrust for thrust as waves of pure, unadulterated pleasure undulated through her. Slick, their bodies slid against each other. Increasing her thrusts, squeezing her vaginal walls, she milked his seed.

"I feel more alive than I ever have." This man was her world, and she snuggled closer. These sensations were too very wonderful. So extraordinary. Humans didn't know how very special they were. She had earned the right to remain human, to stay with Eddie and she'd never stop counting her blessings.

Yearning for more, thrilling to his power, she squirmed in his arms. A growl rumbling in her chest, she raked his back with her fingernails. It was a travesty to cover up such a sexy chest with clothing.

It should be downright illegal.

He rolled onto his back, and then crooked his finger at her. Throbbing and red-hot, his cock aimed at her, sending more delicious shivers through her. "Ride me, honey."

Ooh! Just try to stop her.

Straddling him, she hovered above his cock. Rubbing the tip of it with her swollen labia, spreading her palms over his chest, she loved teasing him.

"You get me. All of me." He bunched his legs, and thrust at her.

Anticipating his move, she stood on her knees, parrying his stroke. "Eager, aren't we?"

"Vixen." He growled and sat up, lunging for her. Circling her waist with his magnificent hands, he pushed her down onto him.

Sliding down on him, she took every lovely, excruciating inch into her heated folds. So hot, so thick, so excited, she quivered uncontrollably. And then, he was bucking under her, pumping into her fiercely.

She upped the ante, tightening her muscles around his girth. Squeezing her thighs against his, she coaxed out his seed. Leaning over him, she tickled his chest with her nipples as her long hair cascaded down, covering them.

Curling up, he captured a tingling breast in his mouth and sucked hard. He kneaded the other nipple between his fingers, bringing her to the brink of orgasm.

Heaven!

Moans coursed up in her and she writhed. A volcano exploded in the pit of her stomach, rocking her. Psychedelic colors swirled around her when she squeezed her eyes tightly.

Eddie's hands clamped around her and she wiggled against him. With a final hard plunge, he filled her and held her tightly against him, his magnificent strength vibrating through her.

Groaning, he trailed liquid fire down her neck with his soft lips. Pulling her down onto his chest, he crushed her to him and snaked his arms around her. "I'm an incredibly lucky man."

She licked her lips. "I'm an incredibly lucky cat...*woman*."

A growl rumbled deep in his chest and he pressed his lips to her throat, driving up her blood pressure again. He rolled over taking him with him, and murmured against her lips, "Sex kitten. And I don't mean cat, either."

About the author:

Ashley Ladd lives in South Florida with her husband, five children, and beloved pets. She loves the water, animals (especially cats), and playing on the computer.

She's been told she has a wicked sense of humor and often incorporates humor and adventure into her books. She also adores very spicy romance which she also weaves into her stories.

Ashley welcomes mail from readers. You can write to her c/o Ellora's Cave Publishing at 1056 Home Avenue, Akron Ohio 44310-3502.

Also by Ashley Ladd:

Enjoy this excerpt from
Civil Affairs
© Copyright Ashley Ladd 2004

He pulled back with a growl. "I don't want your pity."

She smiled at the dear, silly man, as her eyes adored his beloved face that was still heart-stoppingly devastating despite a five-o-clock shadow and lean cheeks. *Well, perhaps because of the sexy stubble.* She wondered how it would feel against her soft flesh...between her legs...

A heat wave rippled through her hotter than the most sweltering Delta day. It was all she could do to quell the rampaging desire and not ravage him right here on the couch. "Pity's the last thing I'm feeling," she said with a wicked wink. A little anger remained, but was rapidly being drowned by red-hot desire. Pity didn't begin to enter the mix.

But she had to know why he was here now. Obviously not to ravage her. There was no matching passion in his eyes. "So, why the change of heart? Why are you telling me now?"

Anger glittered in his eyes as he turned slowly and painfully towards her. "I heard you were in trouble..."

"So you pity me," she drawled and scooted away from him. *Priceless.* He could feel sorry for her but she wasn't allowed the same consideration.

He followed her, trapping her against the end of the couch. "It's not pity. Can't a man want to protect his woman?"

His woman? Tingles raced down her spine and she wondered if she had rightly heard him. She didn't want to be jumping to conclusions. Then the rest of his words registered. "And vice versa? Can't a woman want to support her man?"

Danny stared at her for a long time while she held her breath. "What good would a one-sided relationship be? We have to take turns being strong for the other." What man wanted a shallow, self-centered partner? *No man she could truly love or respect.*

She tried another argument. "Do you want a clinging vine, or a strong woman who loves you?" Since long before the Scarlett O'Haras, southern women had been a hearty lot and she was proud of her heritage.

"Would you want a bitter, whimpering man?" Unmistakable bitterness laced his voice.

"No," she shot back, lifting her jaw high.

"Then you wouldn't have wanted me how I was all those months I was laid up. I had enough pity to make up for everyone. My only redeeming virtue, I thought, is that I wouldn't be bastard enough to subject you to it. Not now, and certainly not forever. I didn't want you to end up a miserable wretch like me. I didn't want you to wake up one day and hate my guts and loathe your life with me."

"That could never happen." Immense love swelled in her heart as she cupped his rough cheek in her palm adoring the feel of it. At great risk to her heart, she admitted, "You're my sunshine. You're the stars and moon in my heaven. You always have been." She moved her hand to his heart. "It's what's in here…" she touched his injured leg tenderly, "Not here, that I love."

A mischievous twinkle lit Danny's eyes and he looked down at the swelling in his pants. With a sly grin, he said Soto Voce, "So you don't care about what's down there?"

Her gaze followed his, and a tingle shot straight to her core. "Don't go twisting my words. I like that *very* much."

He pressed her back against the arm of the couch. "Only *like*?"

She quickly amended her error as she gazed deeply into his darkening passion-glazed eyes. "I love it. Better?"

"I think you'd better show me." His hot breath fanned her neck and then he licked it sensually. She trembled as wild fire blazed through her veins and she could barely stand, her knees were so weak.

Enjoy this excerpt from
As You Wish
© Copyright Myra Nour 2004

Once upon a time, long ago in a land far, far away, there was born a girl of extraordinary beauty. Her parents named her Amira, meaning Queen, because she was so lovely and they hoped her future would shine as brightly as her physical appearance.

Fate was not as kind to the fair maiden as her parents had prayed. Her silken, gold hair, delicate face, and slender form drew the attention of not only those who truly loved her, but the unwanted attention of a powerful, evil sorcerer. The wizard Bakr desired the fair maiden and wooed Amira with words plucked from a dead poet's heart, and the finest silk woven by spiders, creatures created with his magic. His final gift was a breathtakingly beautiful rose carved by trolls from blood-red rubies dug from the Earth's belly.

Alas, the fair maiden was in love with a handsome youth named Omar. Being kind in spirit, Amira turned Bakr down gently, but a scorned sorcerer is not to be reckoned with, and the earth trembled as the wizard's anger spewed forth violently.

Bakr strove to create a unique and cruel punishment for the fair Amira, turning her into one of the djinn. She would not be an ordinary djinn, like those who granted three wishes of a new Master, moving on to a new owner each time they were fulfilled. Amira would be forever condemned to stay with a Master throughout his lifetime, fulfilling his or her deepest, darkest sexual desires.

Every djinn is governed by rules, set forth by the Master djinn, Hadji. A powerful sorcerer may succeed in changing the edicts slightly, as Bakr did, adding one specifically tortuous command. Amira was compelled to watch the fulfillment of her Masters' sexual desires while she was forever denied physical release, unless it came by her own hand.

Throughout the endless centuries, Amira lived alone in her lamp, serving countless self-centered Masters, and long ago sickened by their lustful, selfish fantasies. Oftentimes, sorrow overcame her and she dared to dream of the day a caring Master would release her from eternal imprisonment. The fair maiden wept through the centuries and millennia, her tears sparkling like splintering diamonds dropped from a dragon's eye. Would any Master ever fulfill her wish?

"So…you grant me three wishes?"

"No," she shook her head, sending her silken ponytail swishing back and forth. "I grant your wishes as long as you are my Master."

"Really." Nick rubbed his chin. "This is starting to look up." Staring at her lush curves, his thoughts flew here and there. "All right, I wish for a million dollars." He tapped the palm of one hand. "Right here."

"Oh, I'm sorry, Master. I can only grant certain kinds of wishes."

"Wait a minute, you're setting conditions. I thought I was the Master," he chuckled.

"You are." She executed a graceful bow of her head and upper body. "But I am restricted by rules."

Folding his arms, Nick stared at her. "This sounds fishy, but go ahead, give me the bad news. You're probably going to tell me I can only use my wishes for the good of mankind, or maybe I can't wish for things like material gains."

The genie sighed softly. "I wish that were so, Master. I can only grant your sexual desires."

"My sexual wishes?" Nick stared hard at her. Was she serious?

"Yes." Her lovely face was totally serious.

As he leaned back into the couch, Nick's arms gripped his body tight in a self-hug. Congratulatory. She could grant a life-long dream come true? "You're not kidding, are you?"

She shook her head in the negative.

"Anything I wish sexually?"

"Yes," she whispered.

Man, how many of his hot dreams as a youth had been filled with imagining a genie at his disposal? Lots.

Nick's mind was a whirl of possibilities. Any sexual desire? He had so many. He had already managed to fulfill sexual fantasies many men only dreamed of, but still, there had to be some that were out of even his reach. His thoughts latched onto the potential. Finally, his mind was spinning with so many erotic images he had to take a break.

Shaking himself mentally, Nick zoomed in on the very bizarre reality of a genie standing patiently, awaiting his sexual desires. He realized she was the most beautiful woman he'd ever laid eyes on, and he'd known plenty. Those amber eyes matched perfectly with the golden hair that caressed the slender waist. Even her skin matched, with its golden-brown glow. She was a golden goddess.

Suddenly, he knew what he wanted. He wanted to see his genie naked. See if the curls covering her pussy were as golden as the rest of her. He wanted her.

Going up and down her form with his eyes, he could find no fault with the firm, round breasts that were exposed above the low cut bodice of the pearl-trimmed harem top. Her curving waist flared into womanly hips, and he bet her butt was as inviting as her breasts.

Finally his eyes came up to her golden ones. "My wish is to fuck you."

Why an electronic book?

We live in the Information Age—an exciting time in the history of human civilization in which technology rules supreme and continues to progress in leaps and bounds every minute of every hour of every day. For a multitude of reasons, more and more avid literary fans are opting to purchase e-books instead of paperbacks. The question to those not yet initiated to the world of electronic reading is simply: *why?*

1. *Price.* An electronic title at Ellora's Cave Publishing and Cerridwen Press runs anywhere from 40-75% less than the cover price of the <u>exact same title</u> in paperback format. Why? Cold mathematics. It is less expensive to publish an e-book than it is to publish a paperback, so the savings are passed along to the consumer.

2. *Space.* Running out of room to house your paperback books? That is one worry you will never have with electronic novels. For a low one-time cost, you can purchase a handheld computer designed specifically for e-reading purposes. Many e-readers are larger than the average handheld, giving you plenty of screen room. Better yet, hundreds of titles can be stored within your new library—a single microchip. (Please note that Ellora's Cave and Cerridwen Press does not endorse any specific brands. You can check our website at www.ellorascave.com or

www.cerridwenpress.com for customer recommendations we make available to new consumers.)

3. *Mobility.* Because your new library now consists of only a microchip, your entire cache of books can be taken with you wherever you go.

4. *Personal preferences are accounted for.* Are the words you are currently reading too small? Too large? Too...**ANNOYING**? Paperback books cannot be modified according to personal preferences, but e-books can.

5. *Instant gratification.* Is it the middle of the night and all the bookstores are closed? Are you tired of waiting days — sometimes weeks — for online and offline bookstores to ship the novels you bought? Ellora's Cave Publishing sells instantaneous downloads 24 hours a day, 7 days a week, 365 days a year. Our e-book delivery system is 100% automated, meaning your order is filled as soon as you pay for it.

Those are a few of the top reasons why electronic novels are displacing paperbacks for many an avid reader. As always, Ellora's Cave and Cerridwen Press welcomes your questions and comments. We invite you to email us at service@ellorascave.com, service@cerridwenpress.com or write to us directly at: 1056 Home Ave. Akron OH 44310-3502.

THE
ELLORA'S CAVE
LIBRARY

Stay up to date with Ellora's Cave Titles
in Print with our Quarterly Catalog.

TO RECIEVE A CATALOG,
SEND AN EMAIL WITH YOUR NAME
AND MAILING ADDRESS TO:

CATALOG@ELLORASCAVE.COM
OR SEND A LETTER OR POSTCARD
WITH YOUR MAILING ADDRESS TO:
CATALOG REQUEST
C/O ELLORA'S CAVE PUBLISHING, INC.
1337 COMMERCE DRIVE #13
STOW, OH 44224